The Gilded Mirror

Vesuvius Rising

Jocelyn Murray

ISBN: 1-4801-4667-6
ISBN-13: 9781480146679
Library of Congress Control Number: 2012916674
CreateSpace Independent Publishing Platform
North Charleston, South Carolina

Dedication

For Justin

Chapter I

EARTHQUAKE. Anna Moore braced herself as another tremor shook the town. She was hiding under a table in the shop of an outdoor marketplace, hoping her pursuer would not find her. She could see the robes and sandaled feet of the people walking by. She waited there, willing her heart to slow its pounding. She forced herself to breathe more slowly so she could calm down. How did she get herself into this mess, she wondered? She needed to free her friend Cassius. She had to find him and help him escape without being caught herself.

Anna Moore had stepped back in time again through the gilded mirror that was tucked away in an unused room in her grandmother's house. It was a large antique mirror with the mysterious ability to transport her back in time. It hung on a wall in a darkened room under a large white sheet which did little to keep away the dust. She had discovered it by chance one day when its glass gave way as if inviting her in, and impulsively she had stepped through its ornate golden frame, where it had whisked her back to seventeenth-century England at Corfe Castle on an adventure she would never forget. This was the second time she had stepped through the gilded mirror.

As another tremor rocked the table above her, an earthen jar crashed to the ground, its jagged shards strewn before her. Anna stared at one of the pieces, its bold red paint the color of blood. She stared, and her thoughts roamed back to the gilded mirror that had brought her to this forsaken place only four days ago, whisking her back almost two millennia in time. It felt like an eternity since she had stepped through its frame. Would she ever see it again?

Four days earlier. . .

"Soon I'll have my driver's license and I'll be able to drive myself, Mom," Anna said as she handed the car keys to her mother Beata. Anna was getting ready to go to her grandmother's house. She was an only child who often visited her grandmother, even staying over on the occasional weekend. She was very close to her and loved to listen to her grandmother recount amazing stories about the countless trinkets and artifacts that filled her beautiful Victorian home. A long time collector of antiques, her grandmother was an infinite source of information and wisdom that she wove into the captivating tales that kept Anna spellbound.

"Hmm. . ." her mother frowned, taking off her reading glasses and carefully cleaning the lenses before slipping them into a protective case. Although Anna was a responsible fifteen-year-old, the thought of her driving a car did not sit well with her mother. Images of accidents and hospitals filled Beata's mind. She worried for the safety of her only child. It was not really Anna's behavior that concerned her, but rather all the other people who might come into contact with her daughter. After all, the world can be a dangerous and unpredictable place. In an instant, everything can change. She just wanted to protect her daughter from harm, as any parent does.

"Come on, Mom, please let me drive now. Baba only lives five blocks away," Anna pleaded with a hopeful smile. "Five blocks," she nodded encouragingly.

Beata was gathering some papers to take with her to her appointment. She was a curator at a natural history museum. Anna's father, Robert Moore, also worked there but was presently away on a dig in South Dakota where his team was excavating relics from the ancient peoples who had once lived there.

Beata paused a moment to appraise her daughter, the sheaf of papers in her hand. At fifteen Anna was growing into a lovely young lady. Her long dark hair was pulled back into a loose ponytail and she wore her favorite blue jeans and navy sweatshirt. She had inherited the same large brown eyes and light olive complexion as her mother and grandmother. Beata looked a lot like Baba. And now as she stared at her daughter, she could see her own mother's eyes staring back at her through Anna.

"Please?" Anna asked again, tucking an errant strand of hair behind her ear.

"Only five blocks, you say?" Beata raised a single eyebrow as she eyed her daughter thoughtfully. Although Beata had been living here for many years now, her voice still bore the elegant traces of a carefully modulated accent.

"Yes, five blocks. Short ones too," Anna looked optimistic.

"Ah. Very well my dear. Then you can walk. They are short as you say," Beata gave her daughter a self-satisfied smile.

"Walk? But I always walk there," Anna looked disappointed, the corners of her mouth dropping involuntarily.

"Or I can drop you off. Besides, walking is healthy."

"Ok," Anna sighed, slumping her shoulders a little. "You can take me."

"Do not be in such a hurry to grow up, Sweetie," her mother smiled as she found her purse and tucked the case with her glasses inside. She understood the eagerness of youth. And she wanted her daughter to slow down. Life was too short as it was already.

Anna grabbed her large tote bag and followed her mother into the garage where they climbed into the sedan and headed for Baba's house.

"Thank you Mom," Anna smiled to her mother and kissed her before stepping out of the car and walking up a flight of stone steps that led to her grandmother's home. Dappled light filtered through the stately trees that surrounded the property, making the flowers appear more like iridescent jewels. She opened the front door with a key and let herself in as her mother backed out of the driveway and drove away. Anna had been given a key to Baba's house when she was twelve. She had proven herself responsible enough to keep one and had never let Baba or her parents down. She closed the door and walked over to a table in the grand entrance where she left her keys and bag.

Baba was not home at the moment and Anna was alone. She had planned to do a little reading for a school project, but did not feel like starting just yet. And as she left her things on the table, her gaze turned to the grand staircase that curved its way up to the second floor. She paused a moment, wondering if she should ascend. But it was only a brief moment. For the gilded mirror that hung in a dark room down a long corridor seemed to call to Anna. It drew her like a magnet. And before she knew it, Anna found herself climbing those steps and walking to the room where the gilded mirror hung.

She opened the door and just stared into the darkness for a few heartbeats. Then she switched on the light and carefully stepped around the large clumps hidden under the white sheets that meant to keep off the dust from the furniture and objects stored within. She did not even bother to open the velvet curtain that draped the room's only window. She walked straight over to the mirror and gently pulled off the sheet that partially hid it.

Dust swirled around Anna as she gazed into the mirror's reflection in awe, allowing the sheet to fall to the floor. At seven feet tall by four feet wide, it was truly splendid in every way. It had an ornate frame that was gilded with a heavy coat of gold leafing. The last time Anna stood in this spot was when she had returned from her journey to the seventeenth century. It had all happened accidentally, really, and had almost seemed like a dream. That was less than two months ago, thought Anna in amazement. Time is a strange thing, she realized. So many worlds, secret dimensions, fathomless planes, and as mysterious and profound as the vast sea. She stood staring at the mirror as all these thoughts swirled through her mind like the dust in the room.

All was quiet except for the ticking of a clock that hung on the wall down the corridor. The room had remained shut against the light and held a stale and musty odor that was not at all unpleasant. It was rather comforting, now that she thought of it. It reminded Anna of some of the rooms at the museum where her parents worked. Those rooms that were used as storage, and held countless boxes filled with strange and unusual artifacts, all wrapped in protective paper and plastic. And as she stared, the mirror seemed to stare right back at her. It was eerie and mysterious in the most wonderful way.

Anna lifted her hand and very slowly placed it on the glass, with her palm open. Nothing happened. Then she closed her eyes and leaned her forehead against it as she exhaled slowly. She had been unconsciously holding her breath in anticipation. And as she released it, her breath clouded the mirror in front of her face. Then she heard something. It sounded like voices. But it was jumbled like a lot of people in a public place. She opened her eyes and turned around suddenly, dropping her hand by her side. No one was there. She even walked over to the room's door and peeked outside into the corridor to see if her grandmother had returned. It was quiet. Anna was alone. Then she walked back to the gilded mirror as a thrill of delight filled her veins and coursed through her blood. Once again Anna placed her hand on the glass. As she stared into the mirror this time, the reflection changed. She saw what appeared to be a busy outdoor marketplace with a lot people. And when she peered closer the glass gave way and disappeared. Without pausing to think, Anna took a deep and expectant breath, and stepped over the frame into the unknown world that lay within.

Chapter 2

Anna stopped short after stepping through the gilded mirror. She stood there for a few moments without moving. Then slowly she turned around. Her jaw dropped when she saw her reflection. She was wearing a long belted tunic in a lilac color with two matching hairbands that were secured over a loose bun, and leather sandals with straps that wound about her ankles. The tunic was sleeveless, exposing her slender arms. One golden armband encircled her left arm, just below the shoulder. Another thinner bracelet hung about her right wrist. Tiny clusters of gold and pearls hung from her ears.

Anna stepped up closer to the mirror to study her reflection, her eyes wide with wonder. Her costume reminded her of the ancient Greeks and Romans. Had she stepped back into ancient times, she wondered? She stared a little longer, looking past her reflection and into the room in her grandmother's house from which she had come. It was draped in white sheets to protect the furniture and valuables stored there. Then slowly the room disappeared. It just faded away into nothing and vanished. She was left looking at herself in the glass, and the reflection of the room where she now stood.

Anna turned away from the mirror and looked at her surroundings for the first time. She was standing by a wall in a large open chamber. Tall stone columns soared high above the marble floor, all the way to the lofty ceiling. There were statues of what appeared to be different gods. They gazed boldly at the empty spaces around them from their raised platforms. Some looked like they were carved of stone, while others had been made of bronze. And in the center was a larger marble statue of a woman in a tunic and cloak. Her clothing was carved in a manner that appeared to drape loosely over her head and body. In her right hand she held a burning torch. The flame was painted in a thick layer of gold. Gold also embellished her hair and parts of her clothing. She bore painted jewelry on her form as well. On the dais where she stood was an engraving chiseled into the stone. Anna bent down to peer more closely. It read VESTA.

"Oh..." Anna whispered aloud. "This must be a temple. An ancient temple. Perhaps even of the Roman goddess Vesta." Anna gasped in sudden recognition. "Not Greek, but Roman..." She remembered that Vesta was the Roman goddess of the hearth and home. Perhaps she was somewhere in the ancient Roman Empire. Anna roamed around astonished, taking everything in. The whole structure was colonnaded, reminding her of some of the museums she had visited before. They had housed various Greek and Roman artifacts and statues. And as she continued weaving through the columns, she found the intricately framed entrance.

She stepped outside the double doors under an elegant portico supported by massive pillars. A triangular pediment rested above its decorative lintel. There were steps leading down to a paved stone terrace. Below was a kind of altar. It was very elaborate, decorated in marble carved motifs and a relief depicting a sacrificial scene with a bull. Anna shuddered at the thought of the sacrifices held there, wondering about the animals that had spilled their blood. Incense burned in a brass votive on top of the altar. It smelled sweet. And as she leaned closer to inhale its woodsy fragrance she caught a glimpse of people moving about. They too wore tunics in varying colors similar to hers.

Anna left the altar and its lonely temple behind, where its cold stone gods stared at nothing. She made her way on the paved street towards the people. She walked passed a few women carrying offerings, probably on their way to the temple. They did not even glance her way. She continued walking towards the open marketplace she had spied in the mirror. It spread out beneath the shade of a colonnaded gallery that framed the perimeter of a large open space.

"A forum," she mumbled under her breath. She recognized the layout from her books on ancient Rome. "Of course," she said again, as it all made sense to her. She was standing in the forum of an ancient Roman province. She recalled how the forum was the political, commercial, and religious center of the town. She had just come from one of its temples and now had entered the public square where beautiful monuments rose proudly, lining its borders. The architecture was stunning. A basilica occupied one side, its thick rounded arches supported by heavy carved pillars. A recessed dome gleamed above. A few men mulled about its entrance in serious discussion, their long tunics bright in the sun that seemed to bleach everything upon which it shone. Maybe they were orators or lawmakers, thought Anna as she noted the thick purple stripe that bordered their white togas.

Her gaze roamed to the peddlers that pushed their rumbling carts along the town road, and the marketplace where merchant stalls displayed a variety of wares for sale on tables or hanging from a rod in the entrance. It was a bustling place with crowds of people walking to and fro, carrying baskets, earthen jars, food, or other goods. Mules and donkeys hauled wagons laden with supplies, while cats skirted the paths discreetly, and dogs sniffed the air around them, their tails wagging happily. Small taverns and bars dotted the perimeter and the delicious aroma of food wafted on the breeze. It sort of reminded Anna of the piazzas of modern day Italy. There were children running about at play, and pigeons pecking at crumbs on the ground next to magnificent fountains that sprayed shimmering streams of water.

"Oh!" Anna gasped, wide-eyed, as she collided into someone. She had been too preoccupied with her surroundings to watch where she was going. The boy dropped the load he had been carrying in his arms with a startling clatter. Rolls of parchment skins and small earthenware vials fell to the ground, scattering all around them.

"I am so sorry!" Anna immediately bent down to help him collect the things that had fallen.

"It is alright," the boy replied as he squatted on the ground and reached around Anna to pick up one of the parchments, "nothing appears to have broken." He managed to retrieve all the vials which had miraculously remained intact. Their little stoppers also stayed in place, keeping whatever filled them inside. But Anna frowned, slumping her shoulders and biting her lip in embarrassment, feeling very clumsy for not paying attention while she was walking.

"Here you go," Anna said sheepishly, handing him two of the vials that had rolled by her feet. "You need something in which to put them all."

"I know," the boy shook his head and clenched his jaw as though berating himself. "I would have brought a basket but I did not think I would need one. These things are for my father. We do not live far from here."

"Perhaps I can help you with this," Anna offered with an apologetic smile. Something about the boy inspired her to trust him. "Maybe I can help you carry these things. If you don't mind, that is. It is the least I could do after bumping into you this way."

"Very well," the boy shrugged and laughed. "I could use the help. One moment..." He left the items in a neat little pile on the ground next to Anna while he walked over to a shopkeeper's stand. Handing the man a coin, he took a basket and returned to fill it with the vials. "That is better, yes?" He smiled in satisfaction as he stood with the basket. "Serves me right. I should have come prepared. I am only too fortunate that none of the vials broke. They are for my father, as I said. He is a painter." The boy looked at Anna a moment, tilting his head with a thoughtful expression on his face. Then he leaned forward, holding out his hand.

"We should introduce ourselves. I am Cassius. Cassius Atticus Vitus. Son of Claudius Atticus Vitus. You have heard of him, yes? The painter."

"Anna Moore," Anna shook his hand. Cassius looked to be close to her age, probably about fourteen. He was slightly shorter than she, with black curly hair that grazed the tops of his shoulders. His olive skin was tanned to a golden brown, and he had dark green almond-shaped eyes with light specks that reminded Anna of sea foam. He was handsome in that awkward way that bordered adolescence. He wore a white short-sleeved belted tunic that stopped above his knees, and leather sandals with lots of straps.

"Anna Moore," Cassius said, saying her name for the first time. "You are not from here." It was a statement. He squinted his eyes a little as he tried to mentally place her accent.

"No."

Cassius waited for Anna to continue, but she said no more. She honestly did not know what to say. How could she say anything about the gilded mirror? Remembering the mirror, she glanced back towards the temple that was set farther back from the forum. She needed to remember where it was. Cassius followed her gaze, wondering if she were lost.

"Are you lost, Anna Moore?" Cassius lifted his eyebrows slightly.

"Just Anna," she replied. "Call me Anna. And yes, I think I am lost." It was true after all. She really did not know where or *when* she was.

"Are you alone Anna?"

"Yes I am. My parents are far away and I do not know when I will see them again." The truth always seemed to work best. Why bother making up a story when the truth was most convenient?

Cassius tilted his head a moment as he came to a decision. "Then why not come with me?" He handed her the parchment scrolls while he carried the basket with the vials. "If you do not have a place to stay, you can stay at my house. My parents would not mind at all. We have plenty of room, and it is just the four of us: my father and mother, and my younger sister," he smiled, urging her along. "Welcome to Rulaneum," he announced gallantly, straightening up and squaring his shoulders as though she had already accepted his invitation. Then he began leading the way before Anna could even reply. But she did not really mind. She had made a friend.

Chapter 3

"Where is Rulaneum?" Anna asked. She had never heard of it. But then there were many ancient towns that no longer existed in the twenty-first century. Their names had faded away into obscurity. They walked past a narrow gate, exiting the forum, and down a road paved with large stones. Cassius paused to look at her with a quizzical eye, probably wondering how she got so lost that she did not even know the name of the town.

"It is very close to Neapolis. Less than a quarter day's journey northeast of Neapolis. You have heard of Neapolis, yes?" He raised his eyebrows expectantly.

"Oh yes. Neapolis. Of course." That was the Latin name of Naples. Ancient Naples, in Italy. Anna was glad to finally have a clue about where she was.

"Good," he said, nodding in approval. That was a start. They passed other people heading into town. The street was lined with some shops, taverns and workshops. There was a bakery on one side and blacksmith on the other. Farther down was a fullery where people were busy cleaning cloth. Anna wrinkled her nose as they passed it. It smelled bad.

"What are those pots used for?" Anna pointed to several earthenware pots that sat outside its entrance, as well as others that lined the streets.

"For urine," Cassius explained. "Urine is collected and used in the fulleries to help remove the grease from cloth."

Yuck, Anna thought to herself. The thought of recycling urine made her grimace. Amazing how she had come to take the modern conveniences of her own time for granted. Simple things like laundry detergent were a luxury.

"Who does that? The cleaning, I mean." Anna could not imagine someone actually wanting to work with that. It was too gross to think about.

"Slaves," Cassius replied casually. "Slaves do most of the work." He glanced at Anna again with a slight frown, probably wondering where she had come from. "Do you not have slaves where you live?"

"No," Anna replied a little too quickly. Cassius looked surprised. "I mean *we* don't. My family does not have slaves." She thought of the housekeeper that came once a week to clean her parents' home. She was the same woman who cleaned Baba's house too. But she wasn't a slave. They hired her through a cleaning establishment. It was a job that she got paid to do. She had been working for her family for several years now.

"Really," Cassius narrowed his eyes, wondering if Anna might be a slave herself. Maybe that was why her family did not own any slaves. But her clothing was too luxurious. And she wore expensive jewelry. She also behaved in a manner that spoke of her education. She was poised, and her mannerisms elegant. No. She could not have been a slave. He just shrugged the thought away.

"We do have help, but paid help," Anna added. "There is a woman who cleans our house. But she is paid," Anna emphasized.

"Ah," Cassius replied, nodding his head, a bit more satisfied. A *freed* slave, he reasoned silently to himself. After all, some slaves were allowed to earn money and buy their freedom. Perhaps that was the case with the woman Anna referred to. So they paid her. Some of his family's slaves were paid as well. Especially the more skilled ones, like his father's assistant Antius.

"What sort of painting does your father do?" Anna changed the subject.

"He paints murals. He is renowned throughout the region and his talents are highly regarded and sought after. Sometimes he travels far on painting commissions. Those that hire him are wealthy. The aristocracy or others of the privileged class, like politicians and military leaders."

They passed some wayside shrines that dotted the streets. They were decorated with paintings of the gods to whom they were dedicated. In front of the shrines stood a public fountain. They also passed a large two-story apartment complex called an insula. This was where the commoners lived. The lower levels were used for shops and businesses, while the people lived upstairs. Wealthier people lived in large single-family homes called domus which could be found scattered throughout the town and alongside the insulae, rather than in separate neighborhoods.

"I often accompany my father on his commissions. I am his apprentice." The note of pride was evident in his voice.

"You must be talented." Anna had always like sketching and painting, but she lacked the talent for it.

"I am learning," Cassius shrugged. "My father is finalizing the details of another commission. He is preparing to leave very soon. I will go with him, of course."

They neared the entrance of a house and Cassius stopped. It was plastered in white with a red-colored panel that ran along its bottom and stretched several feet high. Its carved wooden double doors were embellished with bronze studs and door knockers bearing the head of a lion. False square columns flanked its sides, and an elegant architrave crowned its entrance.

"This is your house?" Anna raised her brows, taking in the beautiful details of the doorway. She was impressed.

"It is," Cassius smiled, "this is home. Follow me please, Anna," he gestured with a tilt of his head as he led the way inside.

They entered the doors and through a passage that opened up into the atrium. Two large barking dogs immediately ran up to Cassius, their tails wagging contentedly. They looked like German shepherds. Anna stepped back involuntarily. Why did dogs always seem to catch her off guard?

"Sit," Cassius commanded them in a stern voice. They quieted down and sat attentively at his feet, their tails twitching with the effort of self-restraint. "They only look ferocious," Cassius winked at Anna as he scratched them behind the ears. Anna just watched from a respectable distance. "But they are harmless. At least to us." He laughed at his own words, especially when seeing their effect on Anna. She looked like she was poised to bolt. Then he clapped his hands and the dogs took off.

With the dogs out of the way, Anna felt more relaxed and had a chance to get a proper look at her surroundings. The atrium was a large and impressive room. Colorful murals portraying mythological scenes were painted on all the walls. At its center was a sunken shallow pool that was built right into the floor to catch rainwater from above, where the roof opened up and light streamed to fill the airy space. The pool was inlaid with glass mosaics that shimmered beneath the water, and had a shaft that went down to the cistern below, where the water was stored for household use.

An elaborately sculpted table rested at one end of the pool. A small shrine of marble, about the size of a writing desk, stood farther back against one corner of the atrium where candles were lit in an offering to the Roman gods believed to protect the home. It looked like a miniature-sized temple with its carved architectural and mythological motifs.

Doorways on either side of the atrium led to the bedrooms. A lattice-work screen on the opposite side of the entrance led to a passage where the dining room and kitchen were found.

"Cassius." A woman entered the atrium from one of the bedrooms. She was elegant in her long saffron tunic and black curly hair which she wore pinned up loosely. A few of the long dark curls framed her face gracefully. Anna recognized her smile. It was the same as Cassius. But her eyes were blue. She turned them now on Anna.

"Mother, this is Anna. Anna, my mother Antonia," Cassius introduced them with a gesture of his hand.

Anna smiled and held out her hand, which Antonia took into both of her own. Antonia's face shone with a genuine warmth that Anna liked at once. She was beautiful. Anna glanced at Cassius. She could see a resemblance, but not in the eyes. He had her mouth and her dark curly hair. Just then a young girl aged six or seven, in a white knee-length tunic, skipped into the room. She was holding a small brown ball made of compressed wool tightly wrapped in leather. She stopped short when she saw Anna, and regarded her with curiosity.

"You are very welcome to our home Anna," Antonia said with an open smile. "This is my daughter Julia." Antonia draped her arm around the young girl and drew her closer.

"Hello," Julia said shyly. She looked a lot like her mother.

"Hello Julia. Is that a ball?" Anna pointed to the toy.

"It is, yes," Julia's eyes brightened. "Do you want to play with me?" She began tossing the ball lightly back and forth between her hands.

"Not now," Cassius interjected. "Anna has only just arrived. Besides, I have Father's supplies, the ones he had me get this morning."

"Father is packing," Julia said. Cassius exchanged a quick glance with his mother.

"Is he? Did he get the commission Mother?" Cassius placed the basket on a small table by the wall. Then he took the scrolls from Anna and left them by the basket. The house did not seem to have very much furniture.

"He did get it. He is in the garden now if you wish to speak with him. I am sure he will want to tell you all about it, especially as you are to accompany him," Antonia gestured towards the lattice screens.

"Come Anna, come meet my father." Cassius led the way through the screens. They passed a small kitchen hanging with pots, pans and various cooking implements. Anna could see two women in simple linen tunics working at a counter over a brick oven that was built right into the wall. Slaves, probably, thought Anna. It was a strange thing for her to see people that were slaves.

Anna also saw the dining room with its large angled couches leaning against the walls. They were covered with colorful cushions and surrounded a small round table. People reclined while eating here. They did not sit up in chairs as we do, thought Anna. How peculiar. It seemed uncomfortable to Anna. No wonder that custom was abandoned long ago.

Anna heard a deep voice giving someone instructions from outside. They had stepped out into a garden and under the shade of a colonnaded peristyle. It reminded Anna a bit of the pergola in the backyard of Baba's house. Anna's eyes followed the stone columns that stood like guards in a row, side-by-side. The beams that rested above them hung with vines that tumbled down the pillars gracefully. Everywhere grew lush varieties of colorful flowers, shrubberies and trees. The ripe scents of the plants, soil and flowers blended into a delicious, heady perfume. The garden was adorned with statues and a small fountain in its center. Low hedges lined some of the walls of the gardens, and behind them rose cypress trees like sentinels on the lookout. The walls were painted in colorful outdoor scenes that gave the illusion of a larger space. Anna wondered if Cassius's father had painted them. They were in a similar style as the murals inside the house. The grounds were absolutely gorgeous. No wonder the ancient Romans prized their gardens. They were sanctuaries.

"We leave tomorrow!" Claudius announced happily as Cassius and Anna approached. He held some rags and brushes in his hands, and had just dismissed the young man with whom he had been speaking before Anna and Cassius arrived. So that was where Cassius inherited his eyes, thought Anna, as she studied his face. The father of Cassius was an unconventionally attractive man. Something about the way he spoke and carried himself seemed to command one's attention. He radiated energy. His sun-creased face was tanned to a deep olive brown. Unlike Cassius, his hair was straight and cropped short. It was peppered with lots of gray streaks, especially around the temples, and had receded back with age so that his balding head shone golden under the sun. He was not a tall man, but was built strong and stocky. He looked like a Caesar, thought Anna, at least how she imagined the emperor to be. All he needed was a laurel wreath on his head.

"Really, Father! Then you got the commission!" Cassius embraced his father.

"I told you I would, my Son," Claudius said with a wink. Then Claudius turned to Anna.

"Father, this is my friend Anna," Cassius introduced them.

"Welcome, Anna. Any friend of Cassius is always welcome into our home." Claudius took Anna's hand and kissed it lightly on the back, bowing his head slightly. Anna was immediately charmed.

"Thank you Sir."

"Please call me Claudius."

"Thank you Claudius," Anna smiled.

"Tell me about it, Father. The commission," Cassius said eagerly.

"Did you get my supplies?" Claudius asked, wiping his hands on his toga. He wore a knee-length tunic that was covered in paint smudges. Maybe this was like a painting smock that he donned while working.

"I did Father. They are inside the house."

Claudius nodded and began talking as he walked over to a table by the wall of the house that was shaded by a portion of the roof. Cassius followed behind him, stopping to retrieve more of the rags and brushes that Claudius had placed in an earthenware pot.

"It is for one of the elite guards of our new emperor Titus Flavius Vespasianus," Claudius paused to give more instructions to the young man he had been speaking to earlier. "These are to be cleaned and packed also, Antius. But pack them separately from the others please," Claudius said in a lower voice. The young man looked like he might also be a slave, thought Anna.

"His name is Marcus Servius Attius," Claudius continued, turning back to face his son, "and he is a prefect of the Praetorian Guard."

"The Praetorian Guard!" Cassius gasped, wide-eyed.

"Yes," continued Claudius proudly, "he serves under Titus himself as one of his bodyguards." Claudius looked at his son who was clearly impressed. Anna was too. But she was busy trying to place Titus in history. Where did he fall in among the ranks of all those emperors who had ruled the mighty Roman Empire? Claudius had said the emperor's name was Titus Flavius Vespasianus. So he must have been one of the Flavian Emperors. The Flavian Dynasty had ruled during the first century AD, if she remembered correctly. Wow... the first century... Anna was awestruck.

"And we leave tomorrow. At first light. He has a second house by the sea. He purchased it recently for his wife and has been doing renovations. He wants me to paint the walls of his atrium. Perhaps even in his garden as well." Claudius was gathering some more supplies into a basket that sat under the table on the floor. He was always moving about and doing something. He had that restlessness and energy that made it difficult for him to stand still. And his natural bent for leadership was the kind associated with people in command.

"By the sea?" Cassius asked.

"Yes, south of here. A day's journey perhaps." Claudius handed Antius his basket. "Please be sure to include these things along with the rest, Antius," he said to the young man, "and the things that Cassius brought as well." Then turning back to Cassius he said, "You did buy the parchments, yes?"

"Of course, Father. They are inside with the vials."

"Ah. Very good. Inside then, Antius," he instructed. Antius left them and went back inside to fulfill his master's wishes.

"Will Antius go with us?" Cassius asked. Antius was several years older than Cassius, and had been with their family as a paid slave for about three years now. Because he was close in age with Cassius, they sometimes spent time together chatting or going out on errands when Claudius could spare him. He was treated well, as were all the slaves of the household. Unlike some people, Cassius's parents were very kind and generous with their slaves, treating them almost like members of the family.

"Of course. He usually does. I will need the extra help, although Marcus did mention that I will have the help of his own slaves who live there. But Antius knows exactly how I like my brushes and paints prepared. I do not want to waste precious time teaching one of Marcus's slaves. And you will be busy with errands and getting me any items needed from the town there." Claudius glanced at Anna a moment and paused. That drew Cassius's own attention too. Anna looked at both of them, wondering what her role would be, or if she would even be allowed to go along with them. She wanted to accompany them. It sounded exciting. And time was not a problem. She had plenty of time.

When Anna had gone on her first adventure through the gilded mirror, she had discovered that time had stood absolutely still back home. Although she had spent weeks in seventeenth-century England, no time had passed in the twenty-first century while she had been away. It was as though someone had stopped a clock from ticking. And when she returned home, it resumed exactly where it had left off.

"May I go with you?" Anna asked suddenly. She knew it was probably not polite to ask, but she really did want to go. And besides, unless she did ask, the idea of inviting her along might not even enter their minds. Cassius looked at his father expectantly. He wanted him to say yes.

"And what of your family, Anna?" Claudius drew his brows together in concern.

"They will not mind at all," Anna replied. She began picking at her fingers unconsciously. It was a bad habit of hers, but mostly done out of nervousness, really. She looked at the ground a moment where a black beetle lumbered across one of the paving stones. Then her thoughts roamed back home to her parents. Would they really not mind if they knew? Or would they be too worried for her safety? They would probably be too worried. Of course they would. But they did not even exist yet, Anna rationalized. Almost two thousand years stretched between them. It felt vast and immeasurable. Time was indeed a strange thing. She still occupied space on the earth, but in a different time. It was an enigma to her, a concept that she could not quite comprehend no matter how much she grappled with it.

"Very well," Claudius replied, regarding Anna a moment with a tilt of his head. But he looked uncertain.

"I can help Cassius," Anna added. She was determined to make herself useful so that Claudius would not regret allowing her to go. Cassius beamed. He was happy to take his friend along. The hard part about being his father's apprentice was that he did not have much time to make friends. Especially when they traveled away on commissions.

Anna spent the rest of the afternoon accompanying Cassius on errands. It was fun to walk through the cobbled streets and watch the people go about their work. Stepping back into time through the gilded mirror brought history alive with all the sounds, sights and smells of a world that would otherwise remain intangible on the pages of a history book.

"Anna?" Cassius angled his head, giving Anna a sidelong glance. "Your parents..." he began hesitantly, "they will not mind if you come along with us? Are you certain about that?"

Anna looked away a moment as she thought about how to respond. She saw two children chasing each other through the street, an old man walking with a dog by his side, and some women standing by one of the wayside shrines. They passed a bakery and the aroma of fresh baked bread filled the air. Anna's mouth watered.

"My father is away on work. He also travels a lot like your father does. And my mother sometimes accompanies him."

Cassius said nothing. He thought about this for a moment. Anna could see that he was not convinced, and so she continued, "I visit my grandmother often while they are busy or away."

"You are not really lost, are you." It was a statement. Cassius looked down at the street.

"No. I am not lost," Anna shook her head.

"You are running away?" Cassius raised his eyebrows, looking back up at Anna's face. Perhaps that was it. Sometimes people ran away.

"Not precisely. I am just exploring," Anna was fidgeting with the fabric of her tunic. She kept pulling at the belt nervously, not knowing exactly how to answer. "I just wanted to get away for a little while and see things. That is all. I will return home eventually." She looked up at Cassius. "They will not miss me, I assure you. They will not even notice that I am gone." And that part was certainly true. As far as her parents and Baba were concerned, time stopped. No time would pass, so they really would not miss her at all.

"Very well," Cassius responded, kicking at a small pebble on the road. "We shall have to convince my mother, or she will find it strange." They walked inside the bakery and Cassius purchased a loaf of bread. He handed the man there a coin in exchange for a loaf that was hot and fragrant. As they stepped out, Cassius tore a chunk of the steaming bread and handed it to Anna. Mmm, thought Anna as she savored the first bite. It tasted wonderful. It was more flavorful and textured than the bread at home. More rustic.

"I think we will have to tell my mother that you are running away," Cassius spoke around a mouthful of bread. "That is really the only explanation she will believe. We can just say that you are running away for a little while. Otherwise I do not see how we can convince her," he paused to wipe the crumbs from his mouth with the back of his hand before continuing. "She is very understanding and supportive, but she is also very astute. If there are any chinks in your story, she will expose them at once. But that is only because she is caring and concerned. Sometimes too concerned, I think," he took another bite. "But that is just how my mother is." Cassius looked more satisfied. He had been wondering how they would handle Anna's arrival. His father was not difficult to convince because Claudius was the kind of man that was often preoccupied with his work and his own thoughts. But his mother was another story. She was very intuitive and perceptive. Antonia was the kind of person who could see right through people.

Anna thought the explanation was pretty good. Perhaps it really was not very far from the truth. Although she knew she was not running away. She loved her family and her life. But she was a curious person. And since she had discovered the gilded mirror, her curious nature and penchant for adventure and exploration had grown.

"Perhaps you are right. I hope she believes me." Anna took another piece of the bread from Cassius. He was munching with more enthusiasm now that he felt this problem was settled. But Anna was not as sure. They would know soon enough when they returned to his house.

"Hmm..." Antonia pursed her lips together, and narrowed her eyes. She was thinking about what Cassius and Anna had told her. They were all reclining on the couches in the dining room where dinner had been served. A platter with cheese, olives, flat bread, grapes, chicken and eggs lay on the center table, and the three of them were lingering after most of the meal had been consumed. Julia had left a little while ago with her nurse after she had finished eating. And Claudius had excused himself after Julia so he could attend to the final arrangements of their journey tomorrow.

Antonia dipped a piece of her bread into a dish of red wine. She looked at Anna now, her jaw set. She seemed to be arriving to a decision in her mind. Anna kept her eyes on the food. She could feel Antonia studying her.

Anna was at an age when arrangements for marriage would have been made for her by her father in ancient times. Perhaps that was why she was running away, thought Antonia, for a "little while" as they had explained to her. Maybe Anna wanted to buy herself some time before being forced into an arranged marriage. Anna would have to leave her own family and go live with that of her husband, as was the custom. Antonia could sympathize with this. She regarded Anna thoughtfully with a tilt of her head as she took a sip of wine from a goblet. Her own marriage, after all, had also been arranged. And she was just fourteen at the time. Fortunately, she and Claudius had been a good match and loved and respected one another. Not all arranged marriages were so fortunate this way.

"Very well," Antonia continued. "But you will need more clothing and things of your own," she looked at Anna. "Am I correct in assuming you did not bring anything with you?"

"No. I mean yes. You are correct. I did not think to take anything with me, actually." Anna looked at the tunic she wore, running her hand absentmindedly along the soft fabric that rippled along her form as she reclined on the couch. Stepping through the gilded mirror was not something she could really plan for. It was not like going on a planned holiday and taking a suitcase. It was bit more complex than that. When she had stepped through the golden frame, it was with a deep breath and a blind faith. Yet that was part of the appeal of the gilded mirror. It was exciting and totally unpredictable. It seemed to test Anna's courage and ability to adapt.

"Then you will come with me after our meal. I have some things you can wear and take with you. I will help you pack, yes?" Antonia smiled at Anna.

"Thank you so much, I would really appreciate that," Anna replied. And she *was* grateful. She was also very much relieved that Antonia had believed their story and given her blessing. Anna had been very nervous especially after what Cassius had told her about his mother. But it had all worked out very well, thought Anna with a sigh of relief. It was nice to meet people who were genuinely kind and generous. They were like precious gems in a sea of pebbles.

Chapter 4

Anna felt someone nudge her. She had been asleep, dreaming that she was swept up in a crowd of people that moved like a river when she bumped into something. Only it wasn't in her dream. Someone really was nudging her awake.

"Anna," Antonia whispered. She was bent over the low cot where Anna was fast asleep under a woolen blanket. "Anna," she whispered again, a little louder. Julia was asleep in the room next door and Antonia did not want to wake her. Claudius and Cassius were already up and preparing for their departure.

"Mom," Anna mumbled. She stirred and turned around, opening her eyes suddenly. And when she saw Antonia hovering inches from her face, she nearly jumped out of bed.

"It is alright, Anna. Do not be afraid. It is I, Antonia. The mother of Cassius. Remember?"

The events of the previous day came rushing back into Anna's mind like a flash flood. She sat up at once in bed, holding the blanket closely.

"Antonia?" Anna asked groggily. It was very dark and the narrow slit of a window cut high on the wall did little to let in the murky light of dawn.

"Yes. It is I." Antonia lit an oil lamp and the flame's glow cast a feeble light throughout the plain room. Then she placed it on a table. It was the only furniture in the room besides the bed and a small trunk. "You must get up now, Dear. They are preparing to leave." Antonia laid some folded garments on the foot of the bed. "These are for you to wear now. I brought you a long cloak as well because it is a little cold outside. You can drape it over your head and around your body. It will keep you warm. The sun has not yet risen."

"Alright, thank you." Anna was still very sleepy. She waited a moment as Antonia left the room and closed the door behind her. Then she stretched, got out of bed and dressed.

Cassius and Claudius were already outside with Antius when Anna joined them after saying goodbye to Antonia. They were finishing up strapping all their baggage and supplies to the mule that would be accompanying them on the journey. Antonia had wrapped some bread, cheese and dates in a cloth for Anna to eat along the way, but she wasn't hungry yet. Then the four of them departed on foot with the mule trailing behind them.

"You slept well I hope," Cassius said. He was munching on a piece of flat bread of his own which he washed down with a sweet mixture called mulsum that was made of watered-down boiled wine and honey from a leather flask. Then he handed the flask to Anna but she declined with a polite shake of her head.

"I did sleep well, thank you," Anna replied. "I cannot remember when I last slept so soundly. But I had so many dreams." Not much was said for a while as they made their way along the cobbled road in the shadows of the early dawn. Even Claudius was quiet, as he retreated deep in his thoughts, the cadence of their stride lulling them all into a comfortable silence.

The road stretched for miles it seemed. Anna recalled learning about how the Romans were great builders. Their buildings, temples and houses were splendid architectural masterpieces, built as strong as they were magnificent. And their roads were no less impressive, spanning many, many thousands of miles. They walked on one of those roads now, and Anna kept glancing at the huge stones which paved the way, feeling strangely surreal. It felt a bit like a dream. And as the dawn brightened and the sun rose higher, chasing away the morning gloom, she and Cassius withdrew from their silence and chattered on incessantly.

They made their way south and east of Neapolis, stopping a few times to rest, eat, and water and feed the mule. And as the hours passed and the sun crept westward across the sky, Anna caught her first glimpse of the sea as it shimmered under a heavy sun. They were moving along a bit faster now that the road dipped and snaked its way through and down some hills overlooking a bay by the ancient Sarnus River.

"Ahh..." Claudius exhaled a deep breath in wearied contentment as they paused and admired the view. He stretched his arms high above him to loosen the kinks from the long day. The scenery was breathtakingly beautiful. Rows and rows of vineyards grew on the foothills of a mountain, their lush tangled vines heavy with succulent grapes. There were many orchards and plots of farmland. The verdant fields were speckled with flocks of grazing sheep. And the water from the bay reflected the late afternoon sun like a puddle of liquid gold spilled over its surface.

The harbor's jetties stretched out over the port in the bay, the base of their heavy stone arches lapped by the water where they disappeared below the sapphire depths. Columned shrines that looked like small temples were built on some of the jetties or above the rocky shore, as were domed gazebos, so that seafarers could meditate or make offerings for safe passage to the gods.

Carved statues atop fluted pillars ringed the harbor, standing to welcome the ships that drifted into the port, or those that were anchored by the quay. Fishing boats dotted the calm waters, their painted hulls cheerful in the light. Most of the sails on the boats were furled and fastened with thick ropes, now that the day's work was done.

Anna could smell the sea borne on the breeze that stirred through her hair. She closed her eyes and inhaled deeply. Something about the sea was simply enchanting–its refreshing briny scent, pungent at times, its breeze that seemed to wash through the soul, its vast and fathomless depths that overwhelmed the senses. Standing before it was humbling. It was timeless and true.

"We are almost there," Claudius announced. They were fatigued from the hours of walking. Anna glanced down at her sandals. What she wouldn't give to be wearing her sneakers right now. The sandals gave little support to her aching feet, and she could feel a few blisters forming from the chafing of the straps.

"A nice long soak in one of the baths will cure that," Cassius said when he saw Anna flexing and curling her toes in the leather sandals. She smiled back at him tiredly, thinking about how luxurious a hot bath would feel right now.

"And you said that your father travels much on commissions?" Anna shook her head in disbelief. No motorized transportation existed in this day and age. People got around the old-fashioned way, on foot. She could not imagine walking so far all the time. This made the walk from her own home to Baba's house seem like nothing by comparison. She kind of felt embarrassed and ashamed now that she thought of it. She made a mental note not to ever complain about that again. Her mother would certainly appreciate that.

"This is not so far, Anna," Claudius piped in, overhearing her comment to Cassius.

"But it is not so close either, Father," Cassius said. Claudius just laughed and mumbled something about how they did not know what the word far really meant. He had been on commissions that required many days of travel, a few taking him over a week to arrive. This was nothing.

As they approached the seaside town that rested on the lower slopes of the mountain, they passed by an aqueduct that channeled the water to the people from the hills. The aqueduct stood high above the ground like an endless bridge with its massive stone arches. And nearing the fortified wall that enclosed the town, the little group with their mule walked by the tombs of the town's occupants that lined the main roads. The stone structures clung with moss and lichen that emphasized their age like the patina of verdigris on bronze. They were strewn with weeds, pottery shards, and other discards for which the living no longer had any use. The state of dilapidation and neglect was at once sad and macabre. Anna shuddered involuntarily against a chill.

They entered a narrow gate into the town and continued on the road that was now flanked by houses and large two-story apartment blocks with various workshops, bars and taverns on the street level, and the private sleeping flats above on the second floor. It was very similar to the insulae of Rulaneum. Anna observed the people walking through the streets, their olive skin tanned by the coastal sun. This town seemed much bigger than Rulaneum. She was rather impressed with the order of it all and how it was divided into neat blocks connected by the paved streets, much like the city blocks of her own time in the twenty-first century. The Romans were quite enterprising and industrious.

"House of the Fountain," Claudius said, "that is where we are going." He continued leading the way, and seemed to have recovered from his earlier fatigue now that they had arrived.

"Have you been here before, Father? Do you know where the house is?" Cassius asked. His eyes were bright with an eagerness to go and explore the town.

"Not since the last earthquake here in the year 63," Claudius replied. "That was before your time, Son," Claudius glanced back at Cassius, "sixteen years ago."

Anna's ears perked up. She did the math in her head, quickly adding sixteen years to 63. Let's see… that makes 79. Hmm… she thought. So she *had* been right. She had stepped back into the first century! AD 79. Amazing.

"Much is still in disrepair," Claudius continued as they walked on the sidewalk next to the paved road, their mule in tow. "If you look more closely you can see those structures that were affected." Claudius pointed to a water column that had partially crumbled, its rugged top left idle except for the two seagulls that were perched there now. "They have piped water supply as we do in Rulaneum, but it suffered extensive damage. At least their pipes are in working order again," he gestured to the streets, under which ran lead pipes that carried the water throughout the town. "That was one of the first things they sought to repair." Claudius scratched the back of his head as he walked, observing the town with a thoughtful scrutiny. "Some of the wealthiest houses here have their own private baths with running water. They do not have to rely solely on the use of their cisterns. But they pay dearly for it in taxes, of course," he shrugged.

"And what of the House of the Fountain?" Cassius was curious. "Do they have a private bath?" Anna certainly hoped so. She did not wish to bathe in one of those public bath houses. The thought alone made her frown.

"Yes they do have a private bath. In fact, House of the Fountain is one of those that suffered much damage from that earthquake in 63."

The smell of food drifted out of a tavern and Anna's stomach rumbled in protest. Hers was not the only one. Cassius looked inside and Claudius paused to give Antius direction.

"Have them feed and water the mule while we have a bite to eat. I do not think any of us can resist, especially Cassius here," he glanced at his son with a knowing smile as he handed Antius a small leather coin pouch. Antius led the mule to a nearby stable and left him in the care of a boy working there, giving him a coin from the pouch. Then he joined the others in the tavern.

"Marcus Servius Attius probably purchased the House of the Fountain at a much discounted price," Claudius picked up the conversation from where they had left off on the street. They had stopped at the tavern for a meal. "From what he told me, he has done much to it already in the way of renovations.

It was vacant for years before he bought it. Its original owners moved north after the earthquake. They did not wish to invest the time and expense in rebuilding. So I imagine Marcus got it for a good price. He is a wealthy man and his wife has a taste for luxury." Claudius was happily sharing the information about the house where he was commissioned and both Cassius and Anna listened attentively as they ate. They were curious to know more about it and its owner.

"Will he be there, Father?" Cassius was finishing his stew, dipping a piece of bread into the sauce and eating it. They were seated at a table with a stone bench that abutted a wall. The tavern was small, filled with the smells of cooking and the noise of laughter and conversations of its patrons.

"No. Marcus is in Rome, as is his wife. But his chief slave is overseeing the restorations. Didius. That is his name, I think." Claudius paused to take a long sip of red wine from his goblet.

Anna had finished her meal and was happy to sit down and do nothing for the moment. The long day of walking, and now the meal, had made her a bit drowsy. It felt good to just listen quietly.

"He is an architect, Didius is, or some such thing by profession," Claudius explained as he gestured with a wave of his hand. "From the east somewhere. At least that is what Marcus said," he wiped the corner of his mouth and continued talking after taking another bite of food, speaking with his mouth full. "Marcus spoke very highly of him. 'A capable and talented man,' was what he said," Claudius's eyes narrowed and focused on a corner in the room as he tried to recall something. "No. It was 'a *highly* capable and talented man,'" he nodded, satisfied with himself for having remembered correctly. He took another sip from the goblet and leaned back against the wall, looking at his son and Anna. "But look," he said, standing up suddenly, as though recalling something important, "I am being terribly rude. Poor Anna here is falling asleep while I prattle away about nonsense."

"Oh no," Anna sat up in her chair with a start, "I am fine. Just a little tired is all." Cassius laughed and said he was tired too–tired of waiting any further. He wanted to go see the House of the Fountain so they could get settled for the duration of their stay here.

With the mule following they walked another block and turned down a side street that took them to the front entrance of the House of the Fountain. It was situated on a slightly elevated piece of land that edged the town. It had a similar floor plan as that of Cassius's house in Rulaneum except it was grander and included a second story with a balcony. It was named for the magnificent fountain that graced its garden beneath a huge arbor carved entirely of marble with statues of mythological creatures in playful poses.

All the houses here were almost identically built, and very similar to those in Rulaneum. The House of the Fountain's formal entrance was like Cassius's home with its ornate façade, double doors and entryway that opened up into a grand atrium with a sunken pool that lay under an opening in the roof, ready to collect the rainfall from above. It too had lattice doors that led to a kitchen and dining room, as well as the slaves' quarters. Beyond that was the garden.

Didius had met them at the door and taken them on a tour of the house and garden. A dog was barking outside. He stood up and growled a little when they stepped into the garden. He was a large mastiff with a chocolate brown coat. Didius said something to the dog and he fell silent, his watchful eyes trained on their little group. Anna was relieved to see that he was chained to a post. Claudius raised his eyebrows and pursed his lips.

"He will have to stay out of the way," Claudius told Didius as he pointed to the mastiff.

"I secured him out here just before you arrived," Didius replied. "He will not be a problem." Didius looked at the dog as he spoke. Claudius just nodded.

The house remained largely unfurnished during the renovations, except for a simple bed, small table, and trunk in each of the bedrooms. The large open atrium was without a shrine. Only a small table stood against a wall. Didius ended the tour with the balcony upstairs. It was shaded by a roof resting on columned arches that gave way to an expansive view. They all stood there now and Anna stared out over the town with its red tile roofs, gardens, monuments, temples, municipal buildings and proud columns. The forum was nearby, and farther to the east she could spy part of the great amphitheater that occupied one of the town's corners. To the west lay the bay, peaceful and calm, under a sky set ablaze by a sun that smoldered just over the horizon. The Bay of Neapolis, she thought with dawning realization, finally getting her bearings. It would be the ancient equivalent of the modern day Bay of Naples in Italy.

Claudius and Didius were pointing out different monuments and things in the distance when Anna caught the tail end of Claudius's words. She had been too lost in the view and her own thoughts to follow their conversation before. Because something about this location was niggling her, like an annoyance she could not quite place. Something about the geographical setting of this town by the bay was familiar, perhaps even historically important.

"Ahh, yes," Claudius said as he breathed a deep sigh of appreciation, his hands resting on the low wall beneath the arches enclosing the balcony, "Pompeii is even more beautiful than I remember it." At hearing his words, a cold fear turned Anna's blood to ice. In that instant, it all came together in her mind. *That* was what was bothering her. There had been something vaguely familiar about this place. Something of historical significance that she could not quite place until now. Pompeii, she repeated silently, her jaw dropping. They were in *Pompeii.* It all made sense to her now, of course. It was a wealthy seaside resort town overlooking the Bay of Neapolis. And then, like the inexorable pull of gravity, her eyes turned slowly north to the foothills from where they had come. And with a growing dread that began to simmer silently within her chest, her gaze crawled up the great mountain that dominated the view, looming just beyond the town and the bay. There was the volcano Mount Vesuvius. Vesuvius rising…

Chapter 5

The volcano stood watching the town like a voracious beast biding its time. No one knew of the danger that lurked beyond the town's fortified walls. Its gates, massive stones, carved pillars and indifferent gods might as well have been built of sand, for all the good they would do in saving Pompeii. All this would be buried in several meters of hardened ash. Buried and forgotten for almost two thousand years.

Anna recalled reading about Pompeii's destruction by the volcano Mount Vesuvius in her history books. It had been nothing but a charred blackened desert, barren and desolate. Even the ancient Sarnus River that ran through the town had forever altered its course after the eruption of Mount Vesuvius. She gazed out over the view, seeing the town with its gleaming columns, mighty basilica, temples and stone structures, not as it looked now under the setting sun, but almost two thousand years hence, broken and heaped with rubble, deserted streets sprinkled with weeds, abandoned houses that lay in ruin, the crumbling relics of once proud structures that paid homage to human ingenuity and innovation. And throughout the excavated ruins, a haunting and lonely echo of silence breathing over the town's ghostly remains.

"You are very pale, Anna," Cassius said in alarm after glancing Anna's way. Claudius and Didius turned to her in concern as well. "Are you feeling alright?" Cassius asked with a sympathetic hand on her shoulder. All the color had drained from her face. And her doe-like eyes–usually curious and smiling–were filled with dread.

Anna just shook her head. She was too overwrought to answer. Too many questions flooded her mind and she couldn't rise above the fear and confusion to answer.

"She must be tired from the journey," Claudius interjected in his fatherly way, draping his arm around her back and turning her away from the view, back towards the house. "Didius, please show Anna to her room. Perhaps a little rest will help."

Didius led Anna back downstairs to one of the bedrooms that flanked the atrium. Last week the walls of the atrium had been plastered in a primary rough undercoat that would adhere to a smooth second coat that Claudius would apply with his paints. The walls were a creamy white that waited like blank canvases for Claudius to begin his work in transforming them into stunning artful masterpieces. But now, in the shadows of the waning light that stole through the opening in the roof above the dry sunken pool, those walls were a grayish-blue, the color of ash. And the dark shadows that smeared across their broad and lofty surfaces reminded Anna of smoke.

Anna fell asleep fairly quickly despite her anxiety. The long day of traveling on foot, the excitement of seeing new places and meeting new people, and the shock of having arrived at Pompeii had just been too much. That night she dreamed of the gilded mirror. She was standing before it in a desert wasteland. It stood upright, suspended on its own, without a wall to hang on. And all around her were tumble weeds, rocks and a hard, dry land that cracked in the arid heat. She just stared into the mirror and it stared right back at her. And as much as she tried placing her hands on its surface, nothing would happen. It only reflected the parched landscape back to her. She kept placing her hands on the glass, moving them about like a mime does on an imaginary wall. Then finally the reflection began to change. She watched, curious at first, as the land lifted, growing larger and taller until a great mountain rose up before her. Then, to her horror, the mountain rumbled and exploded with a furious power. And then she screamed.

"What is it, Anna? Are you alright?" Cassius had come running into the room when he heard Anna scream. Dawn's pale light slanted through the single window that stood high on the wall of the room. Cassius could see Anna's face through the gloom. Perspiration beaded her forehead as she winced, tossing and turning in fear.

"Anna," Cassius whispered again, touching her on the shoulder and gently shaking her. He wanted to wake her from her nightmare.

"No, no, nooo…" Anna mumbled, shaking her head.

"Anna, please wake up. It is just a dream," Cassius spoke louder this time and Anna opened her eyes. She blinked a few times and then sat up at once, rubbing her eyes and looking around the small plain room. It was about the same size as the one she had slept in the night before, at Cassius's house. It too was simply furnished with just a bed, a small bedside table and a trunk for storing linens.

"Where am I?" She frowned in confusion.

"We are at the House of the Fountain. In Pompeii.

Anna gasped, realizing that it wasn't just a dream. "Pompeii?"

"Yes, remember?" Cassius stared at Anna, his brows knitted together, wondering why she was behaving so erratically. "We arrived yesterday." He hoped she wasn't getting ill.

"Oh Cass…" she began, twisting the blanket worriedly in her hands. She closed her eyes for a moment and breathed.

"What is it, Anna? Why are you so upset?"

Anna's mind was working. AD 79 was when Pompeii was destroyed by Mount Vesuvius. She had only recently learned about it in her ancient civilizations class. The volcano had erupted in the summer. It was summer now. And the year was AD 79…

"What's wrong?" Cassius asked again.

"Cassius…" Anna began, but then stopped. She wasn't sure how to proceed. She needed to ask some questions first. Even if he thought she was crazy. Cassius just watched her patiently, a worried expression etched on his boyish face.

"What month is it?"

"August, of course," Cassius looked puzzled.

"And we are in the year 79, right?"

"Yes, of course…" Cassius just stared at Anna, wondering where all these questions were leading. Her long dark hair hung in a tangled mess over her shoulders. It shone dark against the simple white tunic she wore for sleeping.

"Yes," Cassius repeated, "we are in August, nearing the Consualia. That is the harvest festival. It is tomorrow actually. August 21st. Father was talking about it last night after you went to bed. We have been invited to various feasts while here." Cassius's face brightened as he shared the news of the feasts that they would be attending. "And then there is the festival of Vulcanalia on August 23. We celebrate them both at home also."

"The Consualia?" Anna was not familiar with the name, but she did know the importance of harvest festivals in many cultures throughout time.

"Yes, the harvest festival, you know?" Then he narrowed his eyes a bit while he rubbed the back of his neck, wondering if Anna was familiar with it. She had to be. It was a great Roman feast.

"August 21?" Her eyes darted to a corner of the room while she tried to figure out today's date.

"That is tomorrow, Anna. Today is August 20." Cassius shook his head, feeling a little exasperated.

Anna buried her face in her hands for a moment. It was August 24 that Mount Vesuvius erupted. That was four days from now. Four days!

"What is it? You must tell me Anna. I am your friend. Do not be afraid. Are you afraid of something?"

She nodded, pushing back her hair off her shoulders. Then she looked at Cassius a moment. His black curly hair framed his face. He reminded Anna of a young lion, his short mane in the early stages of growth. He too wore a sleeping tunic, and his feet were bare. He must have jumped out of bed in a hurry, Anna realized. She felt a little guilty at having awakened him.

"Is anyone else awake Cass?"

"No. Father sleeps very soundly. I am surprised you did not hear him snoring. He sounds like a roaring beast at times," Cassius mimicked his father and Anna laughed. "You can hear him clearly from across the house, even with the doors closed."

Cassius stood up a moment. He had been sitting at the edge of Anna's bed. "They will awaken soon, if they are not up already. At least the slaves will. They will be preparing the meals." He walked over to the door and peaked out into the atrium. The coast was clear.

"Is anyone there?" Anna whispered. Cassius shook his head and closed the door quietly, then returned to sit down at the foot of the bed to face Anna again.

"Father likes to start early in the mornings. He says the morning light is best for painting. He will work for hours at a time without pausing for any refreshment." Cassius was playing with a loose string on the blanket. Anna got up slowly from bed, smoothing down her tunic. Then she ran her fingers through her hair, brushing it off her face to fall down her back.

"I need to tell you something," she began.

"I gathered that much. Go ahead Anna. It is alright." Cassius moved back on the bed, leaning against the wall. He wondered what could be so important or frightful.

"Something is going to happen, Cass," Anna began slowly pacing on the floor. "Something terrible. Dreadful..." she paused to look at him to make sure he was listening. And he was.

"Go on," he said, crossing his arms over his chest.

"You know that mountain, the large one, just north of here?" Anna pointed to the wall. "The one we saw from the balcony. We passed it when we came yesterday. We crossed west on its foothills."

"Vesuvius," Cassius nodded.

"Yes," Anna nodded gravely, then repeated, "Vesuvius. That one. Cassius," she looked at him again, "it is going to explode. It is going to burst, Cassius." Cassius frowned. Anna continued. "A terrible blast will occur four days from now. On August 24. Four days, Cassius! We must leave. We must go before it is too late!"

"But…" Cassius began, shaking his head. "What are you talking about?" He frowned. "That mountain?" He pointed behind him at the same wall Anna had indicated a moment ago.

"Yes, Mount Vesuvius." Anna's eyes were wide. She wanted Cassius to believe her, but she could see that he did not know what to make of her words or even her state of mind. Maybe he thought she was going insane.

Cassius took a deep breath and let it out slowly. "Anna," he began in a voice that an adult would use with a young child, one who needed scolding. Anna set her jaw. She was preparing herself for his response. She could already see it in his eyes. He did not believe her. "Anna, Anna," he said again in a soothing, controlled and condescending manner that only made her feel worse, "that mountain is covered in vineyards and forests, and olive groves, orchards and farmland," as though that made it harmless. "How could something like that happen?" He gestured, shrugging his shoulders and raising the palms of his hands in a question. "Father was talking about Pompeii last night after you left. It has been here for ages." He scooted forward away from the wall and sat upright on the edge of the bed. "Look at this town," he continued, his back straight. "Would it be so prosperous and attract so many people to live here if it were dangerous?" He shook his head again before going on. "So many of the upper classes and aristocracy have homes here. It is a very wealthy town."

"No, Cassius," Anna drew her eyebrows together and shook her head. She kept running her hands through her hair in frustration. "A wealthy town? Do you really think that has anything to do with it? As though the status of its occupants could decrease the danger?"

"There are many thousands of people living here, Anna. Why would they deliberately choose to come here if it were not safe?" He scratched his head a moment and Anna narrowed her eyes at him.

"Because they do not know of the danger!" She raised her voice. "It is very dangerous here! The great earthquake your father talked about, remember? The one in the year 63–sixteen years ago? That was a sign. One of the early signs, Cass. It was because of this mountain," she pointed to the wall again. Then, tamping down her exasperation, she took a deep breath and let it out slowly, lowering her eyes in regret. "Sorry," she said, shaking her head slowly. "I just want you to believe me..."

Neither of them said anything for a while. They were both lost in their own thoughts. Cassius just stared at the blanket on the bed, his eyes following the colorful lines that marked its pattern. Anna was picking at her fingers nervously. The sound of lumbering carts and people began filling the air outside, and the shuffle of feet and movement from within the house told them that others were awake.

"Listen," Cassius stood up, changing the subject. "Let us get changed. Then we can eat something and see the town a bit. Father needs me to do some errands for him. It will be fun to roam around. It is much bigger than Rulaneum."

Anna nodded and forced a smile. "Alright Cass."

"There is a private bathing room beyond the atrium. You can wash up in there if you wish."

"Thank you. That sounds nice. I will."

Cassius left the room and closed the door. Anna slumped on the bed. She felt a bit numb. Maybe nothing would happen after all. Was she absolutely certain about the dates? Now she was doubting herself. She had come all this way with Cassius and his father. It was not as though they could just get up and leave, could they? She would have to convince them somehow. She sighed and stood up, determined to make the best of the situation. Then she gathered some things and left the confines of her room to find the bathroom.

Chapter 6

Anna felt much better after washing up. All the dust, dirt and grime from the previous day were gone. She dressed in a light blue tunic with leather sandals, and combed her hair with the little ivory comb that Antonia had given her. Then she pulled her hair up and fastened it into a ponytail, and wrapped a matching blue headband around her head as was the custom. Her mood brightened as she stepped out to find Cassius. He was munching on a piece of flat bread with some honey.

"Good morning Anna," Claudius said cheerfully as he followed Cassius out of the dining room. Claudius was already dressed in his painting gear. He wore a simple knee-length tunic that may have been white at one time. It now bore countless smudges of paint, like the many battle scars of a warrior. It was obvious that he was eager to start his work. He loved what he did and it showed.

"We will begin with the northern wall," he said to Antius, who was already mixing a white paste in a medium-sized earthenware pot. Antius sat on a low bronze stool, bending over the pot on the floor, and stirring it with a wooden stick. It looked like he was stirring a cauldron. Hunched as he was over the pot, and intent on his task, he reminded Anna of the three witches in Shakespeare's tragic play *Macbeth*. She bit back a smile as she remembered the witches' ominous words, *Double, double toil and trouble; Fire burn, and caldron bubble.*

"Go eat, my dear. Breakfast is a simple affair. Have something before you leave with Cassius." Claudius was already busying himself with the painting preparations.

After Anna ate some bread and honey, she and Cassius left the house. They were off to get a few supplies for Claudius and to peek around the town. They did not speak of the events from earlier that morning, and proceeded as though it had never happened. But Anna saw Mount Vesuvius as they moved through the streets. It waited in the distance, watching the town in predatory silence.

"We are very close to the forum. Let us go there first," Cassius suggested. They walked along the cobbled streets where people were already busy with their work. Most of the insulae varied in size with the living quarters above on the second floor, and the shops below at ground level, but all were not more than two-stories high. Most of the windows, if they even had any, were built high on the walls as a precaution against thieves and looting. And many of the people owned guard dogs for safety too, just like in Rulaneum, Anna thought. She remembered Cassius's two large German shepherds.

The two-story blocks stretched neatly in many directions, a sweeping expanse of red tile roofs over buildings that were plastered in white, with red paint that ran in a panel along the lower walls. There were some balconies and windows on the second stories with shutters pulled open to allow the air to circulate through the closed quarters. Wealthier homes were interspersed among those of the poor and working classes rather than in separate neighborhoods. And walking along the street, Anna could see the peaks of the cypress trees poking above their walled private gardens. She was impressed with the architecture and layout of the town, including its paved streets and sidewalks. They reminded her of some of the older European blocks that were still around in her own century, and that also had shops built below the living quarters above. It was a very practical and convenient setup for those who lived and worked there.

They passed a public fountain where two women were fetching water. Cassius jerked Anna out of the way of a mule lugging a cart laden with amphorae–large terracotta jars for storing oil and wine. She watched the cart roll by, its wheels following in the deep ruts that were carved into the roads. There were workshops spread along the way that were already open for business, including a bronzesmith, carpenter, and ironmonger, as well as a launderer and fullery. Inns, bars and taverns were open as well and drew a mix of local patrons who lived nearby as well as the sailors, merchants and other foreigners passing through Pompeii on business.

As they entered the forum they joined a sea of faces that filled the public square. A flock of pigeons suddenly rose from the ground in the square's center, their wings beating in a swooshing motion that sounded like the wind as they circled around the forum, probably looking for a new place to land. Above them seagulls swooped in the sky, surveying the ground for discards, while the cheerful song of smaller birds filled the air around them. More shops, bars and taverns stood with their shutters pulled open and tied back for business under the shade of the vast colonnaded gallery that spread beneath the beautiful architecture of the public buildings. It was much larger with many more people than Anna had seen in the forum at Rulaneum. Fishermen carried baskets brimming with silvery-scaled fish, oxen and mules pulled wagons heavy with grain, fruits or vegetables, people pushed carts filled with straw and hay, women balanced terracotta amphorae on their shoulders, or held them closely in their arms.

All through the slow-moving mass that flowed like a river through a gorge, animals weaved in and out of the current in the company of their owners. There were sheep and goats being herded from one place to another, dogs running alongside the wagons, and cats that watched from a safe distance, or slept in the summer sun that shone brightly on everything below.

Cassius and Anna moved out of the flux and towards one of the large fountains in the square. Children were splashing and playing on the ground by the water. Just then a low rumble caught the attention of people everywhere. Some seemed to think at first that it was one of the heavy carts on the street. But no cart could shake the earth this way. Anna locked eyes with Cassius as the rumbling grew stronger. Some pottery fell from their hooks above the stalls where they hung in their stands, crashing loudly on the stone ground. Dogs whined, not knowing where to hide. A few people screamed, ducking under the tables in the marketplace.

"Come!" Cassius grabbed Anna's hand and pulled her towards the center of the forum's open square. "We will be safe here. Nothing can fall on us." Anna said nothing at first. But her eyes were fixed on Vesuvius where it rose above the town, looming like a giant, and dwarfing the metropolis. Even the towering palms and cypresses that soared above the ground seemed humbled by the great mountain's presence.

Cassius followed her gaze towards its peak. It looked velvety from this distance. Its forested and fertile slopes reached gracefully towards the blue sky. Anna saw the doubt in Cassius's eyes. He just could not comprehend how that mountain could be the cause of the rumbling. He had never seen a volcano. In fact, none of the people that made their homes in the towns that nestled between the shores of the bay and the gentle slopes of the mountain even knew what a volcano was. But they were certainly used to the rumbling. Earthquakes were not uncommon in this area, and the tremors that shook the town were largely taken for granted or ignored as an unavoidable nuisance. But it certainly never even entered their minds that it was due to the seemingly innocuous mountain that guarded the borders of their town. And after a few minutes, people resumed their activity as though nothing had happened.

"They get a lot of earthquakes here," Cassius explained, dismissing it with a wave of his hand as though it were nothing. "Father was telling me about the big one in the year 63. Look over there, at the Temple of Jupiter." Cassius pointed to the north end of the forum where the temple rose grandly from its strategically-placed high podium. Like the other temples in the area, and the Temple of Vesta in Rulaneum, it was accessed by a flight of stone steps below massive pillars that held a triangular pediment depicting a scene carved in relief of the Roman gods with Jupiter seated proudly at their center. The portico was topped by carved figures and flanked on both sides by pedestals that once supported equestrian bronze statues.

"See how the horses are missing, and the pedestals are cracked?" Cassius continued, as they both drew closer to the temple. "They were damaged in the earthquake of 63. And look at the columns," he pointed to the pillars of the portico. "They have since been replaced. But you can see the cracks running through the last two. Those have not yet been fixed."

"And don't you think that would be enough reason for us to leave?" Anna shook her head, trying to get through to Cassius. "The town was heavily damaged," she continued. "You can still see it for yourself. Look at the House of the Fountain, for instance. And that is just one among many." They ascended the stairs of the great temple.

As the supreme god of the Roman Empire, the Temple of Jupiter reflected all the grandeur and adulation befitting a king. Anna couldn't help feeling dwarfed by the immense stone structure. And entering the temple, they fell silent when the first thing they saw was the colossal head of Jupiter carved of marble. It lay to one side on the floor, leaning against a column.

"That must have fallen in the great earthquake," Anna whispered to Cassius. He just nodded as they stepped quietly around the enormous head with its long hair, curling beard, and deep-set eyes that gleamed white in the shadows of the temple. The floor of the temple was inlaid in stunning mosaics that stretched out like elegant rugs. And farther back against the rear wall they found a massive foot, a huge mask, and an assortment of fragments, figurines, statues and other relics that lay in a broken mound. Anna shook her head, pursing her lips, "See?" She looked sideways at Cassius, trying to gauge his reaction, but his expression was unreadable.

They left the temple and walked back with the crowd, not really paying attention to where they were going as they meandered along by the shops. "Didn't many people flee?" Anna stepped around a child that was crouched on the floor by a column. He appeared to be waiting for someone, his mother perhaps. A dog sat at his side and the rope that hung on his neck remained tightly grasped in his hand.

"Of course they did, but some returned," Cassius replied, not even glancing towards the child. "They could not just abandon their homes and businesses. Where would they go Anna?" He ran a hand through his curly hair, looking at her as though she should know better.

"But Cass, there were more earthquakes after the big one. And there must have been some before it too, warning them of the danger." They stopped in front of a bar and Cassius handed the old woman at the counter a coin in exchange for something to drink. She poured a thick, pinkish-yellow liquid into two cups and placed them before Cassius and Anna. Anna picked up her cup and sniffed it cautiously. She watched Cassius as he downed his in one long gulp. He must have been thirsty, she thought. Or else maybe he really had been a little afraid after the tremor. If he had been, he hid it well. She drank the mild, sweet liquid. It was similar to the mulsum honey-wine mixture she had tried before at Cassius's house. The Roman's liked their sweets, she thought. It was delicious.

"But earthquakes are one thing, Anna," Cassius put down his empty cup and turned to face Anna as he continued their debate.

"Cass," Anna began, not sure how she would ever convince him, "tell me this: when was the last earthquake here? Strong earthquake. The last one in Pompeii?"

Cassius did not reply right away. He really didn't know the answer to that question. But the woman at the bar did. She overheard them talking and said, "We have not had an earthquake for some years now," she was wiping down the counter with a wet rag. "It has been a while. At least ten years that I can remember. Probably more. And I have been living here since long before you both were born," her eyes sparkled in her weather-creased face. She had to be older than Claudius, thought Anna. She looked to be about Baba's age. A grandmother, perhaps.

"See?" Cassius said, as he looked at Anna with triumph in his eyes. "It means nothing."

"Oh no, young Master," the old woman interjected. "It does mean something. The very fact that it's been so long is that the earth has grown restless again," she removed their empty cups and placed them in a large pot that sat below the counter, then wiped her hands on the apron that was tied around her tunic.

Cassius shifted from one foot to another as the woman's words grabbed his attention. People passing by were talking of the earthquake as well. It was on everyone's mind. But they seemed to carry on like it was nothing, and just a small price to pay for living here.

"Yes, I know," continued the wise woman as though reading both their minds, "people think nothing of it because they are used to it," she nodded her head slowly. "Ah," she continued as she turned her piercing gray eyes towards Anna and Cassius, "is a lion less dangerous because you have seen him before? Or a bear, for that matter?" She narrowed her eyes, nodding again. "Familiarity makes the lion *more* dangerous. Because your guard is down. You are used to his presence, so you think nothing of him. And that..." she paused for effect, wagging a crooked finger and nodding sagely again as she did, "and *that* is when he strikes..." Her words hung in the air between them. Anna felt a chill ripple through her body. She cast a sidelong glance at Cassius, wondering if the woman managed to at least convince him of the possibility of danger. But Cassius said nothing. He stood there motionless, a faraway look in his eyes. For a moment he reminded Anna of one of those fallen statues that stared blankly at nothing.

Chapter 7

Cassius and Anna had spent the day roaming through Pompeii and seeing some of its magnificent sights. The Basilica somehow appeared even grander to Anna than the Temple of Jupiter. Perhaps it was its large nave that felt immeasurably vast. Its classical architecture reminded Anna of the natural history museum where her parents worked. As the center for commerce and political proceedings, the Basilica seemed to seize the attention, drawing the eye to the huge columns that framed its sides, and the coffered marble ceiling that made Anna feel dizzy as she gazed above with her head back, turning slowly to take it all in. Its lower walls were covered in paintings that simulated marble and were inset with real stone moldings. The veneer was exquisite, accentuating the structure's overall prominence, and the prosperity of the town.

As they wandered the streets on their way home from the forum, they passed by a mill where grain was ground into flour. A blind-folded donkey was pulling a wooden stake that was attached to a large cone-shaped basin set into a stone base. Round and round went the donkey slowly, pulling the stake that worked the grain. Then the flour was baked into delicious fragrant bread that enticed those passing by the bakery. Cassius bought a loaf to take home with them.

When they returned to the House of the Fountain they found Claudius standing back and assessing his work with a tilt of his head. In his hand was one of the parchments, and he seemed to be comparing it to the sketches that now appeared on the wall. He was deep in thought and did not even glance up at Cassius and Anna when they arrived.

"Very nice, Father," Cassius said. He stopped to admire the outlines and drawings that covered one of the walls in the atrium. Antius was sorting through some things on the floor and paused to turn and see Cassius's reaction. Cassius smiled at his friend and walked over to inspect the wall more closely. Although he was a slave, Antius was very much valued for his competence and artistic eye, and Claudius had come to depend on him much in his work.

Claudius said nothing for a moment, and just rubbed at his back with his free hand, still holding the parchment in the other. "You need a break, Father," Cassius could see that his father's back was sore.

"That is what I have been telling him," Antius said, as he stood up with a basket of supplies.

"Have you been working all day?" Cassius shook his head in disapproval.

"Of course, Son," Claudius replied. His booming voice seemed to always carry above everything. "That is why we are here." And he laughed at the obviousness of his own remark. "I do not have the luxury of wandering about aimlessly like cattle," he glanced at Cassius and Anna, "not that *you* are cattle, my dears," he quickly added, "but what I do takes time," he formed a hard line with his mouth, nodding to himself, "much time and concentration."

"Even cattle need to eat, Father," Cassius said with a mischievous grin.

"Who are you calling cattle, Son?" Claudius retorted, but he was smiling. Antius bit back a smile and said nothing.

Claudius's humor was infectious. Claudius reminded Anna a bit of an absent-minded professor, always lost in his own thoughts and projects. There was nothing crafty or underhanded about the man. He was as open and honest as he was energetic and talented.

"Dinner is served," Didius said as he stepped into the atrium through the lattice-screened doors that led to the dining room.

"Ah. Very well Didius. Thank you. I shall wash up and join all of you in a moment." Claudius set down the parchment on a small marble table and stretched his arms above his head. Then he left the room, rubbing the soreness from his back as he walked away.

"Tomorrow we go to the amphitheater," Claudius announced after taking a sip of red wine from his cup as they dined. "It is the Consualia. No work is to be done tomorrow." He picked at the grapes from the platter that rested on the small table between them. They were all reclining on the sloping couches that were built into the wall of the dining room. Didius had joined them but only after much prodding and insistence from Claudius. Slaves did not usually dine with their masters, but ate separately in another room. Didius was different. How he became a slave, no one knew. Perhaps he was captured and forced into it when the Romans conquered one of the many lands that now comprised their empire. But he would probably not remain a slave for long. He was very industrious and was most likely saving to buy his freedom as other slaves had.

"There will be much sport at tomorrow's festivities," Didius said. He looked a bit uncomfortable reclining with the others. Anna cast him a sympathetic glance. She was not very comfortable either. It felt strange eating with her hands too. No silverware graced their table.

"With gladiators?" Cassius's eyes brightened at the thought of seeing gladiators fight in the great amphitheater. They were highly respected and revered. The popular gladiators were practically worshipped by the crowds. But Anna said nothing. She had learned about gladiators and the blood sports that occurred in the amphitheater. Killing exhibitions, she thought with distaste. A bloody and violent show.

"Of course," Claudius replied with his mouth full. He was eating a piece of fish fried in olive oil. "What is an amphitheater without gladiators?" He popped an olive into his mouth. Anna picked at her food. The topic of discussion put a damper on her appetite.

"What's wrong, Anna?" Cassius looked at Anna. She was pursing her lips together as a single line marred her smooth brow. She kept playing with the grapes in her hand, rolling them around in her palm.

"I've never seen gladiators," she said, forcing herself to eat one of the grapes. Both Cassius and Claudius took that as an indication of her interest in going tomorrow.

"Then you are in for a real treat," Claudius replied as he took another sip of wine. But Didius said nothing. He just watched Anna quietly over the rim of his cup, his face carefully schooled into a bland expression. He suspected she did not want to go tomorrow. And he couldn't blame her. Such atrocities were barbaric. His own people did not concede to blood sports. But what could they do? When in Rome, one must behave as the Romans. It was not a question of liking what they did, but rather of adapting. And the ability to adapt was integral to survival.

Another tremor shook the ground. While the first one earlier that day gave the sensation of a rolling motion, this one was more of a jolt. It startled Anna and she sat up at once, gasping as Claudius's wine cup fell from the small table onto the floor. Although it didn't break, its contents spilled, staining the floor a blood red. Anna glanced at Cassius who was as wide-eyed as she. But he quickly tamped down his fright and sat up also.

"Nothing to worry about my dears," Claudius looked as relaxed as ever, popping another olive into his mouth. "What a shame though, the wine spilled." But they did not need to wait long for more. Didius summoned one of the kitchen slaves and she promptly returned with a fresh carafe.

"Father," Cassius began, looking a bit nervous, "that was the second earthquake today." Anna could see that Cassius was worried. Maybe he was starting to believe her.

"Tremors are very common in these parts," Claudius explained with a wave of his hand. "Is that not so, Didius?"

"It is," Didius said as he helped himself to some cheese and flat bread. "But there have not been any for years," he paused to take a bite and chew in pensive silence before continuing. "Let me see..." he squinted his eyes, tilting his head thoughtfully as he sifted through his memory. "The last one, I think, was in 67 or 68. More than ten years ago," he nodded to himself. "At least ten years."

"Well," Claudius replied waving away the danger with a flick of his wrist, "we have nothing to worry about. We will not be here that long."

No one will be here that long, thought Anna. Several towns in the region will be obliterated. But she did not say so aloud.

"A week or two, more or less. Perhaps a bit more, depending on whether or not I paint the garden walls," Claudius added.

Anna looked away a moment, recalling the photographs in the books she had seen of Pompeii as it lay in ruins almost two-thousand years later. Only broken walls and faded frescos remained of the town's tidy blocks, their beautiful red tile roofs gone. The towering pillars of the Basilica, and those that stood like sentinels lining the galleries of the forum and under the great porticos were reduced to stumps. The magnificent temples with their elaborate pediments, altars and figurines were crushed down to rubble. The once-gleaming white marble that shone brightly under the Mediterranean sun was now pitted a dingy brown. The gladiator barracks and open palaestra where they practiced and honed their fighting skills had become a tomb for those who died there, housing the relics of their bones, as well as the many pieces of armor and equipment which did nothing to protect them from death. And the amphitheater, that great oval arena that drew hordes of blood-thirsty spectators who fed on the torture and suffering in its exhibitions, now lay fallow, its blood-stained ground overgrown by grass and weeds, and the stone rows that seated about 20,000 people, now just empty fragmented chunks of rock.

"A couple weeks," Claudius repeated. He sat up and took a deep breath, letting it out with a nod. "Like I said," he stood up from the couch, "tomorrow is the Consualia. No one will be working, including the slaves," he paused a moment in thought, then continued, "at least those slaves whose masters give them the day off. Even the animals will rest."

"But what about the horse and chariot races?" Cassius asked before his father left the room. "Won't there be any races? Or will the horses rest as well?"

"Of course there will be races, Cassius. The races are a vital part of the festivities. I was referring more to the beasts of burden. Donkeys and mules and such," he said with an impatient flutter of his hand. "It has been a long day. Now if you will please excuse me." And he inclined his head to them before he turned and left the room.

Chapter 8

Anna was the first one awake the next day at the House of the Fountain. She had been lying awake in her bed for over an hour, and unable to fall back asleep. Dressing quickly, she left her room and made her way out into the garden, walking over to the fountain which was dry during renovations. She ran her hand along the marble. It felt cool and smooth against her skin. Then looking up towards the east she saw the sun beginning to rise. Shades of pink, orange and gold streaked the sky above the tiled rooftops of Pompeii.

But there was something strange about the scene. It was somehow too quiet. Where were the birds she had seen just yesterday and the day before that filled the air with their song and chirping in the trees? Where were the gulls that cried their haunting calls as they swooped through the sky? Where were the pigeons with their blue-gray iridescent feathers reflecting the light of the sun as they roosted in small flocks, pecking for crumbs in the forum and other public places? She had seen them in Rulaneum. She had heard them there. But not now. And that struck her as odd and eerie. Because by this time of morning they would be fluttering about with their cheerful noise. Had they all simply vanished?

The weather was hot and dry, even for August. The sea usually breathed a refreshing moisture that filled the breeze. That breeze seemed to have stopped in its tracks yesterday. The only breeze that stirred the town was parched now. It felt a bit like standing in front of a warm oven after it had been left open from baking. It was unsettling.

"You are up early again," Cassius joined Anna by the fountain. He had tied his hair back into a low ponytail with a thin leather cord. It suited him. His fourteen-year-old face was on the cusp of manhood. Sometimes he looked more grown-up and other times Anna could see the remnants of childhood in the curve of his cheek or the wonder in his eyes. Right now he looked quite young with his hair pulled out of his face. Anna smiled to him with a faraway look in her eyes.

"You are not still thinking about Vesuvius, are you?" He moved to sit on the edge of the fountain, and began drumming his fingers quietly along its surface. He reminded Anna of Claudius at that moment, with that certain restless air.

"Look at the sunrise," Anna responded, ignoring his question for the time being.

"Beautiful," Cassius agreed.

"I love how the sun paints the sky in vivid colors," Anna continued as she gazed towards the east. "It's as though the sky is heralding the sun's arrival. Like a blazing cape perhaps, worn by the sun as he rises. Then he sheds the cape as he moves boldly through the day across the heavens," she tilted her head as she considered the image in her mind. "And then," she straightened up a bit, "the cape is draped around him once again as he sets."

"You *are* still thinking about Vesuvius," Cassius frowned. "I can see it in your eyes." But Anna said nothing for a moment. She just waved his words away. Then she turned to face him.

"Of course I am thinking about it. It *will* happen," she started twisting the end of the cloak she wore around her shoulders. "There will be more tremors first. Stronger ones. And then it will happen. Mark my words."

"What makes you so sure? How do you know this?" Cassius shook his head. He stood up and began to casually kick some loose pebbles that lay by the fountain. Anna had been right about the tremors. And according to Didius and the old woman at the bar that served them yesterday, there hadn't been any earthquakes in over ten years.

"I just know." Anna did not know how else to reply. What else could she say without making him think she was crazy?

"You just know," he repeated dully. "Is that what I am supposed to tell my father, Anna?" He ran his hand through his hair and the leather cord came loose, setting his dark mane free. "He would laugh at us." Cassius bent down to pick up one of the pebbles which he tossed back and forth between his hands. He *was* a lot like his father, thought Anna. Same nervous energy. He had to always be doing something. "I would need more proof of some kind. Saying that you just know is not enough," he shook his head. "It would not be enough to convince him." Then a thought occurred to him. He stood up straighter, holding the pebble in his hand. "Are you..." he began but stopped. He wasn't sure how to ask. "Are you... a clairvoyant?" He shot her a quick glance to gauge her reaction. When she said nothing he rephrased the question. "Can you tell the future?"

"In this case, yes. I can," she nodded. Maybe he would accept that. Maybe posing as a clairvoyant and claiming she could predict the future would convince him. But he laughed. Just a short outburst which he quickly tamped down. Her response had been too uncertain. She did not strike him as the kind who could foretell events. Anna looked away, her face reddening. She felt foolish.

"I just do not see what Vesuvius has to do with anything," he insisted. "That mountain has been there forever. And you come along and claim that it is going to explode? That just does not make sense, Anna. It is one of the most ridiculous things I have ever heard."

"Erupt," Anna corrected, as she turned back to face him after regaining her composure. "It will erupt. Like... like..." she was trying to think of an analogy that he could understand. "You know when bread is baking in an oven? And the dough rises higher and higher? And then the top cracks and splits open. And steam escapes from it," she looked at him to see if he was following. He was.

"Yes. So you think that mountain is going to grow?"

"No. It will split and all the hot molten rock inside will escape."

"I have never heard of such a thing," Cassius replied. Anna realized that no one had heard of such a thing in this age. That was why they lived by the sleeping volcano, totally ignorant of its terrible power. Even the earthquakes did not scare them enough to move away. They simply put up with them, or explained them away as the effects of the wrath of their sullen gods.

"That is just the strangest thing I have ever heard," Cassius shook his head. "And I do not think you should go around telling anyone because they will think that you are not right in the head."

"Hmm..." Anna huffed in irritation, trying to think of a way to convince him. "If I can show you a sign, before it happens of course, will you believe me? Will you try to convince your father and the others to leave while we still have time?"

Cassius looked at her, narrowing his eyes. But then he agreed, "Alright, yes. But it has to be something..." he thought a moment, "something undeniable. A proof that I cannot refute."

"Very well," she replied. Anna pictured the ruins of Pompeii as she had seen them in her history books. She recalled that the town was hit by very strong earthquakes just before Mount Vesuvius unleashed its fury. Many of the people had fled after that. They took it as a portent of evil and destruction and left in a hurry. But others had not. They wanted to wait it out, thinking that the earthquakes would quiet down and leave their town in peace once again.

"The forum," she began as she looked Cassius sternly in the eyes, her shoulders squared. "Several of its columns will crack in the earthquakes and start to fall before the mountain erupts." She knew that eventually all would be reduced to stumps, but damage had occurred just before the eruption. Cassius shook his head, a faint smile touching his lips. But then he said, "Alright, if that happens—"

"*When* that happens," Anna corrected.

"Ok, *when* that happens, I will believe you."

"And you will convince the others? That we need to leave?"

"Yes, yes," he replied impatiently. Then he sighed heavily as though he had been tricked into their bargain.

"You will see for yourself soon enough, Cassius," she nodded sagely. "You will soon understand." Then she took a deep breath and exhaled. "I only hope it is not too late for us. To escape, I mean. I hope it will not be too late," she turned once again towards the sun, remembering the plaster casts of the people who had died in Pompeii. Many of their bodies were contorted in agony, from a death that had sucked the life out of them in excruciating torment. It made her so sad to think of it now. Would their bodies also be among the dead?

"Three more days, after today, that is. Three days, Cassius. And then all of this will be gone. Three days." And she turned and left him there, sitting back down on the fountain with his shoulders slumped, and staring at the sky in gloomy silence.

Chapter 9

A thrill of excitement filled the air as people began celebrating the Consualia that day. Anna was walking along the streets with Cassius, Claudius, Didius and Antius. Most of the slaves in the town had been given the day off to spend with their families, especially after the busy harvest the previous week. Those who did not have any relatives usually enjoyed the holiday with their masters. All the shops were closed, their shutters pulled down and locked against possible looting.

People hung colorful swags of flowers and bunches of herbs on their doors for good luck. Animals were being led through the streets in a great parade, free from their yokes and usual burdens, and exempt from any work, now that all the hard plowing was done. Horses, mules and donkeys wore garlands woven of flowers draped over their heads and around their necks. Even the sheep, goats and pigs wore wreaths as they were herded freely along the roads. Baskets of fresh fruit sat outside the doors of the homes they passed, in an offering of thanks to the gods for a bountiful harvest.

When they entered the forum, it had been transformed into something even more splendid, if that were possible. It was festooned with garlands that encircled the great pillars of the surrounding galleries. Musicians roamed through the streets playing flutes, trumpets and drum-like instruments that enlivened the atmosphere. There were performers with tiny bells strapped round their wrists and ankles, and they tinkled and chimed with the movement of their dancing. Others clapped and played tambourine-like instruments or clinked brass cymbals together joyfully. Plentiful food was handed out freely, and wine flowed generously from great amphorae into the cups of the revelers.

Anna, Cassius and their little group were drawn into the mass of people that moved through the streets in tune to the thrum of the merrymakers. They made their way slowly towards the great amphitheater that waited on the other end of the town. Didius had secured special seating for them on behalf of Marcus Servius Attius. The owner of the House of the Fountain was presently in Rome, probably enjoying a similar spectacle on a much grander scale.

The Consualia honored the Roman god Consus, who was the protector of the harvest and grain especially. As an earth god his altar lay buried beneath the soil where it would be uncovered with great pomp and circumstance on the evening of the festival. This would happen tonight in the great amphitheater. But only long after the performances had been enacted, the races had been run, and the gladiators had fought. Then the final rites would be performed at sunset as the ancient custom decreed, with torches flaming, incense burning and a triumphal procession of offerings that would linger long after the sun had set over the sea.

Anna felt herself jostled through the crowd. They were pushed along the road like a great sweeping current that moved towards the amphitheater. It was too loud to even attempt to carry on a conversation. They had to yell above the din to be heard.

"Cass!" Anna yelled as they were separated by the crowd. She should have been holding his hand, she admonished herself. Now what would she do? Would she be able to find her way back to the House of the Fountain? There was no turning back. Even if she wanted to go back, it was impossible to walk against the crowd. She took a deep breath and braced herself as she was pushed along the streets by the torrent of faces. At least they were all headed to the Amphitheater. Maybe she would find Cassius there.

Suddenly another tremor rolled through the town. But most of the people were too caught up in the celebrations to even notice. Many were dancing through the streets. And in the constant movement they did not feel it. But Anna felt it. She hoped Cassius and the others felt it too. After the surge of the crowd led Anna down another block, she felt someone grab her arm, and to her great relief, she saw that it was Cassius. She took his hand and did not let go until they arrived to the southern entrance of the amphitheater.

"Your tickets," said a guard who stood at the heavy wooden gate under the arched entrance. He was holding a long spear and had his sword sheathed in the scabbard that hung on his leather belt. His bronze helmet shone in the sun. Anna wondered if he might be one of the gladiators.

"The gladiators are in the barracks," Cassius whispered to Anna as though reading her mind. "They will come out later."

Didius handed the guard their tickets and they were allowed inside. They followed Didius to a lower section that afforded some of the best views of the arena. These marble slabs were covered in cushions which made them much more comfortable. But there wasn't any shade. Anna was glad she had brought a light wrap in white linen which she planned to drape over her head when it got hotter. Antonia had mentioned that it would probably come in handy, especially if they would be joining in any festivities. She and Julia were spending the Consualia with Antonia's family who also lived in Rulaneum.

"Fantastic seats," Claudius proclaimed with a satisfied nod as he sat down on one of the red cushions. They were seated just high enough to remain at a safe distance from the combat, and from having dirt kicked into their faces during the competitions and races.

"You have celebrated the Consualia before, yes?" Cassius asked Anna.

"Not like this," Anna replied. Harvest festivals at home often coincided with Halloween celebrations.

"So you have not been to an amphitheater? Ever?"

"No." Anna turned away from Cassius and fixed her gaze on the arriving performers below. They were entering the arena from the northern gate. People were still filling the great stadium, climbing up to find their seats. The performers were making their preparations. Then they began playing music and marching around as more people arrived. Soon all the seats had been filled and the gates were closed. Then a procession of animals were led inside, adorned with floral wreaths. They joined in the parade of musicians while a beverage of water mixed with wine was passed around so that the audience could fill their cups.

The sun drenched the arena in a blaze of heat. Anna draped her thin wrap over her head to keep it from scorching her skin. And as the procession marched around the stadium, and speeches were delivered and prayers said to the gods, another tremor struck. But the people received it with applause, laughing and shouting with joy. They thought the gods were speaking to them, or showing their approval for the festivities.

"Father," Cassius tapped his father on the shoulder, "aren't you afraid?"

"Of what?" Claudius looked perplexed.

"The tremors, Father. There have been several since yesterday."

"It is nothing. Probably just the stomping of the people," Claudius said with a wave of his hand. "If anything, it adds to the revelry," and he turned back to speak with Didius.

"I have relatives here," Antius leaned in to tell Cassius. Anna was seated between Antius and Cassius, with Claudius and Didius on Cassius's other side. "On my mother's side. Cousins of hers."

"And what do they say of the tremors?" Anna asked. She was very curious.

"They say it is a bad omen," he replied.

"Really," Cassius said in his most dismissive voice. He did not believe in such things. And he thought that people who did were not too bright.

"What else do they say?" Anna insisted.

"They say that there were many tremors before the great earthquake of 63. Smaller tremors that led up to the big one. They say that it is happening again. At least they think so," Antius said.

"Do they say anything about the mountain?" Cassius asked him.

"What mountain?" Antius asked.

"That one," pointed Cassius. "Mount Vesuvius. Do they think it has anything to do with the tremors?"

"I do not know," Antius replied as he studied the great mountain with a frown. "I have not heard it mentioned."

Cassius shot Anna a sidelong glance. He had that *I told you so* look in his eyes. She just tried to ignore him.

"Look!" Claudius interrupted them. "The races are beginning!"

Mules had entered the arena, strapped to the chariots they would be pulling. A trumpet sounded and the races began. The people stood and cheered loudly from the benches. Laughter echoed in the stands when some of the mules stopped midway through the race, refusing to continue.

"Hahaha!" Claudius's voice boomed. "Stubborn beasts," he laughed. Two of the riders had fallen off their chariots when the mules had stopped abruptly. One mule turned around and began running in the opposite direction, dragging the empty chariot behind him. And still others moved at a leisurely pace, not bothering to hurry with the rest. It was hilarious. Even Anna was laughing. She stood up to cheer them on. After the race, the mules were rewarded with grain and fresh apples. Flowers were thrown down on the ground before them by some of the spectators. A couple of the mules bent down to eat some of the flowers and the crowd erupted in more laughter.

The horse and chariot races were next. Again a trumpet was sounded, and this time a handkerchief was thrown into the air by a magistrate presiding over the festivities. The race began when the white cloth touched the ground. This event was less comical as the horses ran around the arena, pulling the chariots with their costumed riders. The charioteers looked splendid in their leather helmets, corsets, knee pads and shin pads. Their colored tunics represented the four seasons, each belonging to a separate team of green, red, white and blue. The reins were grasped tightly in their left hands, while they used a whip in their right to urge on their horses. Tucked in their waists were curved daggers that gleamed in the light of the sun. Even the horses looked magnificent in their regalia with their long manes strung with ribbons and pearls.

Unlike the mules, the horses seemed to know what they were doing, and had a keener sense of competition. People in the stands were exchanging coins, betting amongst themselves to see who would win. And when one of the chariots hit a bump, its rider was thrown into the air, falling to the ground with a hard thump. He rolled to one side in an attempt to get out of the way, but not quickly enough. Another horse came stampeding behind him and ran him down. The crowd gasped. The rider was seriously injured. Anna saw the blood streaming down his face. Two men rushed onto the arena from one of the gates, and dragged him to safety. Anna hoped he would be alright. It was just the beginning. More blood would be shed.

As the hours passed and the sun moved across the sky, the mob's thirst for blood grew. The festivities continued with more races and performances. Then it was time for the gladiators' much anticipated arrival. Strange how most of them were criminals or slaves, and yet they were celebrities, clearly venerated as heroes. Anna glanced at Cassius. Both he and Antius had their gazes fixed on the scene below. Claudius did as well. But Didius watched with a look of revulsion, his mouth set in a hard line. He glanced at Anna now and their eyes met for an instant. Anna was glad she was not the only one who did not appreciate the sport, but she wondered about the rest of the crowd who adored such bloody displays of violence.

The crowd had been waiting eagerly for this. A gate was opened and the men filed out solemnly to the raucous applause of the mob. Dressed in leather boots with laces, leather vests over short tunics that bore shiny scales or pleats, they carried heavy swords and shields that caught the sun's light and reflected it back to the crowd. Some wore elaborate crested helmets made of bronze that hid their faces completely. Small holes fashioned out of connecting circles covered their faces as did the flaps that protected their throats. Others carried clubs, spiked flails, or weighted nets and tridents, their sharp prongs gleaming in the sun.

They paraded around the arena in their heavy armor, their muscles taut and glistening with the sheen of sweat that glazed their deeply tanned bodies. Then three horns sounded, trumpeting loudly in succession as another gate was lifted and wild boars charged into the stadium. The crowd roared. People stood cheering loudly, shouting at the gladiators to kill the beasts. Anna felt the tension grow as the people stomped and cheered from above. She did not know where to look. The gladiators had formed a circle facing outward, their backs against each other. Their shields were up and their swords drawn. The boars leaped and stamped their hoofs, growing anxious in the din. Then they turned to the gladiators and charged, their heads lowered, and wicked tusks poised to stab and gore at the men.

The men shouted from their shield-wall, one of their cries a ululating howl resounding above the rest. A hush fell over the crowd as they grew instantly quiet and watched the combat in morbid fascination. Then the slaughter began. Anna turned away, averting her eyes with her hand. She couldn't watch. But she heard the crowd gasp and a sharp intake of breath as they followed the battle with rapt attention. Two of the boars had been killed already. Another lay twitching in its death throes. Then the men split up, fighting in pairs to kill the rest.

One of the gladiators was defending another from the sharp tusks of a particularly large boar. He did not see the second boar that came charging behind him. The crowd screamed a warning but it was too late. The boar buried the points of his tusks in the back of the man's thighs, lifting him up and tossing him down hard on the sandy ground. Then the first boar turned back and charged. He thrust his tusks deep into the fallen gladiator's belly. Another gladiator threw a weighted net over the large boar, stabbing him to death with his trident. But it was too late. The fallen gladiator had been mortally wounded.

One-by-one the rest of the boars were slaughtered. But not before two more of the gladiators were injured. Fortunately their injuries were minor. Anna caught sight of the blood that ran down their legs, staining the ground. No wonder sand covered the ground, she thought. It was meant to absorb the bloodshed. She lowered her head, fixing her gaze on her lap. Then she closed her eyes. She felt dizzy. The hot summer sun beat down on Pompeii mercilessly. All the shouting, blood, and heat were suffocating.

"Anna," Cassius laid a hand on Anna's shoulder.

"I need to use the bathroom," Anna mumbled. She wanted to get out of there. The carcasses of the boars and the dead gladiator were being dragged away through a gate. Then sand was poured over the blood that had spilled, and raked over the ground evenly. People were shouting for more. They waited anxiously for the next bloody spectacle to entertain them. Anna stood up.

"Where are you going Anna?" Claudius asked her. But when he saw her face he understood. "Ah," he nodded. "Antonia is the same. But someone must accompany you." Claudius looked over at Cassius who appeared hesitant. He did not want to miss out on any of the action. He was in awe of the gladiators, as most people were.

"I can accompany her," Didius offered. He too had seen enough.

"Thank you Didius," Claudius said. "Keep the tickets in case the guards ask to check them once again."

"They are safe in my pocket," Didius replied. Then he escorted Anna out of the arena.

Chapter 10

Anna breathed a sigh of relief as they exited the gate. The streets were much less crowded now. Didius led her to the public toilets that stood just beyond the amphitheater and waited outside.

"There you are," Didius handed Anna an apple when she returned. Fruit was being distributed freely in honor of the festival.

"Thank you Didius." The apple was a dark red. Anna took a bite and savored the juicy sweetness. "I think this is just what I needed," she told him as she munched. He was eating an apple of his own.

"You do not care for the sport either, do you?" She asked him.

"Not the blood sports," he shook his head. They were walking by the outer perimeter of the stadium. Neither was in any hurry to return. Besides, it felt good to stretch the legs and move around after sitting all day.

A small tremor shook the ground. Anna stopped suddenly and looked up at Mount Vesuvius. One could see it from almost anywhere in Pompeii. The town rested in the shadow of the great volcano. Didius followed her gaze to the mountain.

"You are not used to the tremors," he stated.

"No, I am not," Anna wanted to ask Didius a few questions. "Didius," she began, "do you know anything about that mountain over there?" She pointed to Mount Vesuvius.

"Only that its slopes are very fertile. The vineyards produce many grapes, and the orchards much fruit." He took another bite of his apple. He was a tall man, younger than Claudius, but not by too much. Anna wanted to tell him about the eruption but she had no idea how to broach the subject. Would he think differently of her if she said something? At least Cassius remained her friend. He did not go denouncing her to anyone.

"You are afraid of the tremors?" He cast her a sidelong glance. "I am too."

"Really?" Anna drew her eyebrows together. Didius did not seem like the kind of person who was afraid of anything. Something about the way he carried himself said that he had endured much in his life, and perhaps even grown a thick skin as a result. He tilted his head in thought, gazing in the distance before them as they continued strolling outside the amphitheater.

"I have already told this to Claudius," he continued. "We were speaking of it yesterday. It has been a while since the last big earthquake. And for some reason, the land here moves much. It is restless, this land is," he said. "And it will probably happen again. The signs are not good. I even said so to Marcus Servius Attius."

"Oh, the owner of the House of the Fountain?" Anna looked at Didius. "The prefect under the emperor Titus?"

"Yes. I advised Marcus to wait. I sent him messages suggesting that he wait on the renovations but he is insistent. His wife is with child and she wishes to come live in Pompeii, away from Rome," he took another bite of his apple and then continued. "We had two tremors before you arrived, you know. Just a few days before you came. But they were very small. It was then that I sent word to Marcus about delaying the work. Because the small tremors usually precede the stronger quakes."

"What happened the first time when the big earthquake struck?" Anna was hoping to make a connection between the earthquake of AD 63 and these tremors.

"It was preceded by smaller tremors, just like now. That is why I am fairly certain that something on a much larger scale will follow," he said. *Oh you have no idea,* thought Anna to herself, *just how much larger the scale will be.* But she did not say so.

"I do not want to stay here, Didius. Something terrible is going to happen."

"I know," he nodded in agreement. "I sense it too. But I cannot go anywhere. My duty lies with Marcus and with the House of the Fountain."

"But there is more..." Anna continued hesitantly, "that mountain–Mount Vesuvius–something bad will happen." She glanced at him to gauge his reaction but he was listening attentively, a serious expression on his face. "The earthquakes and the mountain are related. They are caused by the mountain. It is dangerous."

"The mountain is?" Didius looked at Mount Vesuvius now. It was nearing sunset and its verdant slopes shone a hazy golden bronze. He looked back at Anna but said nothing. Who was he to contradict her? One thing he learned in his life was that anything was possible, and that some things are not predictable or explainable. And so when he heard her words he just nodded.

The blood sports were over at last. Anna and Didius had returned to their seats, joining the others in time for the closing ceremonies. Every year the altar of Consus had been buried within the ground of the amphitheater itself, especially as it would be uncovered with great formality in the presence of the townspeople. And now as the crowd grew quiet, pleasantly lethargic after a long day of celebrations and cheering, the altar was uncovered and removed from its earthen repose.

Just as the sun was setting over the bay and coloring the sky in red, purple and gold, a train of torchbearers stepped out onto the arena where they formed a great circle around the altar. One-by-one the torches were lit in succession so that the light of their flames threw magnificent shadows that undulated over the ground that still bore the blood of the dead and wounded. Then more people filed out onto the arena, carrying incense and baskets of fruit and grain–representing the first fruits of the townspeople's harvests. Musicians wove between them, playing their instruments and dancing until they came to stop in front of the altar. The incense was lit on the altar, while the baskets were placed on the ground, encircling the altar by several meters. Two people lifting a large terracotta amphora then doused the baskets with a very strong undiluted alcoholic beverage made from grapes. Slowly the torchbearers tightened their circle, stepping closer to the baskets that were now drenched in the red fluid. And just after the sun disappeared, sinking into the sea, a horn resounded, echoing loudly through the amphitheater, and the baskets were set ablaze by the fires of the torches.

A loud gasp escaped the crowd as they watched in awe. They were mesmerized by the fire that seemed to dance around the altar. The flames dipped and rose in a rhythm of their own as they consumed the baskets in a great crackling pyre. Anna also was spellbound. The ceremonial proceedings had been glorious. Glorious with something eerie. Perhaps it was due in part to the incense that drifted languidly over the crowd. The smell of incense with the smoke of the fires and the sickly sweetness of the burning fruit blended into a heady fragrance that was simply intoxicating. And as the great amphitheater slowly emptied and the crowds drifted out of its gates, Anna thought of Vesuvius and how the altar of Consus would be buried once again after this night. Yes, she thought with a heaviness in her chest, the altar would be buried again, but this time under the ash of the great mountain.

Chapter II

That night a terrible earthquake hit the town. This was not one of the tremors that most of the people dismissed with a casual wave of their hand. It hit Pompeii with a jolt that was strong enough to awaken the dead, if that were possible. Anna screamed when the walls shook and her bed slid an inch over the stone floor. She jumped out of bed and left her room. She ran out into the atrium where she was joined by the slave women of the house, their faces drawn, shoulders stooped and eyes wide with fright. Soon the rest of its inhabitants came. Even Claudius looked upset as he lit an oil lamp and went to inspect the walls of the atrium. A deep frown etched his brow when he found thin fissures that ran jagged paths across the width of the wall. Then another tremor hit them. Cassius shot Anna a look of fright. She saw that he believed her at that moment. She could see it in his eyes. At least he was afraid of the earthquakes.

"Father, it is not safe here," he began in trepidation. "We must return to Rulaneum." Cassius had lit an oil lamp as well, holding it closely by his chest. The shadows cast by the flame made his eyes seem larger. He had the look of someone who had seen a ghost. Didius and Antius waited in the gloom, looking equally disturbed.

"Do not be foolish," Claudius said as he shook his head impatiently. "Marcus is not paying me to start a job and leave without completing it." They were all dressed in their sleeping tunics–white linen robes that glowed eerily in the light of the lamps.

"But Father," Cassius insisted, raising his voice a little, "there will be nothing left to this town. Broken walls are not for painting." Noise drifted in from the street. They heard people moving about outside, a sense of urgency and fear in their voices. It was the darkest hour of night, just before dawn. Everything always seemed scarier in the dark, thought Anna.

"No," Claudius repeated. "I am not leaving. Besides," he continued, as he placed the oil lamp on a small marble table, "one of Marcus's friends is interested in my work. He too has a house here. It is by the theater. He wants to see my paintings here first." Then turning his attention back to the fissures on the wall he said, "We can patch these cracks Antius," he was tracing them with his fingers, "they are shallow. We can just patch them and continue with our work." He looked more satisfied after seeing that he would not be delayed by the earthquake. "I intend to get that commission. It is a friend on his wife's side. Marcus's wife, that is. And now I am going to go back to bed before the sun rises. You can all mull about here if you wish. I am going to try and get a little more sleep." And he turned on his heel and left the room without another word.

Anna and Cassius were left alone in the atrium after the others had cleared away. Cassius was sorting through some of his father's supplies absentmindedly. Anna could see that he was nervous. "Father wants me to get more pigments for him," he said as he fiddled with a brush. "I think he is bent on impressing the friend of Marcus so he can get that commission as well."

"What will you do?" Anna asked.

"What he says, of course. What else can I do?"

"Your father is fearless."

"Stubborn, actually," Cassius corrected. "But perhaps that is why he is so good at what he does." He walked over to the wall and examined the fine cracks for himself, running his fingers along the wall.

"Because he is stubborn?" Anna was confused. She did not see how stubbornness could be an asset to anyone.

"Because he works hard and does not give up easily," Cassius clarified. "He has never walked away from a commission without finishing it first. He is very good at what he does. But people like him because he completes his work in a timely manner. He is very reliable." He turned away from the wall and took a deep breath. "What good is talent if one does not have the discipline to use it properly? It is like a pot of gold that remains buried in the dirt. My uncle had the same talent, you know," he lowered his voice a little as he confided this to Anna. "The brother of my father. He too is talented. But he is lazy and prefers to lose himself in drink," he shook his head in disapproval. "What a waste. All that talent wasted. My father never intends to follow in his brother's footsteps. And so he is stubborn that way. You can see why now, yes?" He looked at Anna and she nodded.

"Yes, I understand," she said.

"Let's go to the forum," he said, changing the subject abruptly.

"Right now? It is dark still."

"No, after sunrise. Look, dawn is almost here." They stepped outside into the garden and looked eastward at the sky. A faint glow hovered over the horizon, heralding the dawn. "Unless you want to go back to sleep," Cassius added with a smile. He knew very well that Anna would not be able to sleep a wink. He would probably have a hard time convincing her of even stepping into her room after that earthquake.

"Sleep?" Anna looked surprised. "Do you really think I can just go back to sleep after that earthquake? She shook her head. "It is only the beginning Cass. More will come."

"I know, I know, that is what you said."

"Well then."

"Then go dress," Cassius instructed. "I will get us something to eat from the kitchen and then we can leave. The sun will rise soon."

They made their way along the paved streets in silence. Remnants of the Consualia were strewn everywhere. Partially-eaten fruit lay on the sidewalks where the baskets had been the previous day. And the flowers that had adorned the parading animals that had roamed through the streets, and the wreaths and garlands that had festooned the doors, now lay trampled along the wayside or discarded in the gutters, wilting with decay.

Cassius checked his pocket to make sure he had remembered to bring the leather coin pouch to buy the pigments for his father. He seemed to be in a hurry. Anna watched him quietly, glancing his way as they walked. More people filled the streets as the sun began to rise. The delicious smell of fresh baking bread floated through the air as they passed a bakery. Sleepy shopkeepers unbolted the shutters that guarded their wares, then began setting things up for the day, displaying all sorts of goods for sale on masonry or wooden counters, or hanging from the wall, or from a rod on the ceiling.

One shop that carried the large amphorae that was used for wine and oil looked as though a team of oxen had passed through. The ground was strewn with broken pottery. A woman was sweeping the mess out into the street. And as she bent down to pick up one of the shards, she cut her hand. Anna saw her wince as the blood ran down her palm.

"Look," Anna pointed as they passed the shop, "it is from the earthquake. I bet her shop is not the only one with broken things." But Cassius didn't reply. He was too preoccupied with his thoughts.

They turned down another street where they passed several inns, taverns and workshops. One man was bent over an oil lamp from the low stool on which he sat, repairing the handle that had broken off. He was a bronzesmith. All kinds of oil lamps, pitchers, bowls, vases and beautiful artifacts–all in bronze–filled his shop. Like many of the other shopkeepers, he lived in the quarters above his store. Anna saw the wooden stairs that led to the second floor. They rose from a concrete foundation that formed a landing with two built-in steps. His was only one of the many shops that were part of the great blocks that lined the streets. There were shops carrying decorative figurines, painted vases, jewelry and other trinkets for sale along the road. Anna paused to look at one of them, pulling on Cassius's sleeve.

"I just want to have a peek," she told him as she moved towards a jeweler's shop.

"Alright," he said, a bit relieved for the distraction. He had been in a sullen mood since the earthquake. And the lack of sleep after the previous day's festivities did not help much. His green eyes looked tired with dark smudges below them.

They stepped inside and Anna approached a table where a cabinet displayed jewelry. Rings, necklaces, bracelets and earrings in gold and silver, and others inlaid with precious gemstones glittered in the morning light. There were pretty brooches, pins and decorative hair ornaments that were made of glass beads and pearls. Anna looked over everything, stopping to rest her gaze on a bracelet that caught her eye. It was fashioned of thin, bright silver with a delicate pearl-drop pendant. Such a pretty thing, she thought, as she made to leave the shop.

"Wait," Cassius said. He had seen her admiring the bracelet. He recognized the look in her eyes. He had seen that same look in his own mother when they visited the town shops and something special snagged her attention. He had also seen it in his sister when she wanted a new toy. He walked back inside and spoke with the shopkeeper. And before Anna realized what he was doing, he paid for the bracelet and gave it to Anna.

"Give me your wrist," he said. Anna lifted her arm to him and he fastened it for her. Then she wiggled her wrist and the silvery strand sparkled in the sun. It was lovely.

"Thank you Cass," Anna said with a smile. She leaned in quickly to give him a hug. "It is so pretty. I will treasure it always."

"Women and jewelry," Cassius shrugged with a laugh. It was good to hear him laugh, especially after the stressful morning's events.

Anna thought of her mother and grandmother who enjoyed browsing such things. A pang of longing pierced her heart when she remembered them. She missed them so much. It felt like an eternity since she had been home. They did not even exist yet. How strange, she thought, shaking her head.

The first thing Cassius did as they entered the forum was inspect the columns. One-by-one he studied them intently. And sure enough, many of them bore cracks, some of which looked deep enough to topple them over if he pressed on them with all his might. He glanced at Anna a moment, wondering how she knew.

"But they have not fallen, Anna," he said.

"Not yet, Cass." She said no more. She did not have to say anything. Because just then another tremor shook Pompeii. Although it was not nearly as strong as the one that jolted them awake earlier, it seemed to last longer. Anna grabbed Cassius's hand and they ran towards the center of the public square. One of the pillars that supported the portico of the Temple of Jupiter split in two widthwise with a loud crack, and its upper half tilted slightly to the side. Cassius stared in awe, then glanced Anna's way. She too was staring. Although it was still early and uncrowded, a few people were scrambling in fear, not sure which direction to go. Anna heard one of the shopkeepers curse to himself as he pulled down the shutters he had unbolted just a moment ago. He locked up his shop and left without turning back.

"We cannot get the pigments from here," Cassius pointed to the gallery where most of the shops remained closed. "Look, they have not even opened yet. Many probably won't.

"From the earthquake?"

"Most probably from the Consualia yesterday. But Father told me where to go in case one was closed. But it is a longer walk," he shook his head. "What a waste of time," he looked at Anna, "isn't it Anna? We are wasting our time."

"By getting the pigments you mean?"

"Yes."

"We are," she agreed. "He will not have any use for them soon. There will be nothing left to paint."

"But there is no way for me to convince him, Anna."

"So you believe me now?" She asked him. "Really believe me?"

"I do, yes," he nodded. Then he looked away as they continued walking, steering as clear as possible from anything that might fall on them if—or rather *when*—Cassius amended silently to himself, another earthquake should hit. Anna just smiled. But she turned to hide her face so Cassius would not see her and misinterpret it for something else. She did not want him to think that she was laughing at him or gloating. She was just happy that he believed her, finally. Now all they had to do was convince Claudius of the danger and they could go home in plenty of time before the fatal eruption of Mount Vesuvius.

"Why are we bothering to even get the pigments, then? Why don't we just go tell him we should leave?" Anna looked back at Cassius. They were passing a bakery on another street but it was closed. "See?" Anna pointed to the shutters that covered the bakery's entrance. They were locked from inside. "I think some of the people are heeding the warnings. Why else would their shops be closed? You saw that man at the forum close his shop and leave. He was shaking his head and muttering to himself."

"Yes but you must also remember that yesterday was the Consualia. People are probably feeling very sluggish today. They are trying to recover from the festivities," Cassius explained. Anna imagined that many of them *were* probably recovering, especially those that had drank too much of the wine that flowed freely on the streets and at the amphitheater. "Sometimes people take off work the day after a big festival."

"Do you think it has anything to do with the earthquake?"

"I don't know. The House of the Fountain did not seem to be damaged," Cassius answered.

"But all you saw were the cracks in the wall, Cass," she insisted. "And it was dark still. Perhaps not all the damage is visible. Look at the columns we saw in the forum."

"True," he said. "But a lot of the damage was probably already there from the big earthquake in 63. I just think that it will take a lot more to frighten the people of Pompeii enough to leave. This is their home, after all. Where will they go?"

"It is a second home for many," Anna replied. "Like Marcus Servius Attius. He lives in Rome. House of the Fountain is a second home for him."

"Still," Cassius insisted. "They are used to living with tremors. It is like that old woman said, remember? The old woman from the tavern. She said something about a lion being more dangerous when you know him."

"No," Anna corrected, "she said, 'familiarity makes the lion more dangerous.'"

"Same thing," Cassius shrugged. "And the people are very familiar with this lion, it seems."

And soon he will strike, thought Anna as she looked up towards Mount Vesuvius. But she did not say so aloud. Because when she glanced at Cassius, she could see that he was probably thinking the same thing. He too had his gaze fixed on the great mountain.

Chapter 12

Claudius was in high spirits when Anna and Cassius returned. He did not even seem to mind that they weren't able to buy the pigments he wanted. Many of the shops had been closed including those that carried his supplies.

"They are recovering from the Consualia," Claudius said. "I should have known. But it does not really matter now. We will be fine with what we brought," he gestured towards his supplies.

"The walls look much better, Father," Cassius looked surprised.

"That is all Antius's doing," Claudius said. But Antius just shrugged it off as though it were nothing.

"It was easy enough," Antius said. He had patched up the cracks beautifully. No one could even tell that they bore any fissures that morning.

"Easy for you maybe, Antius," Claudius said in his booming voice. "But that is only because you have a talent for this art." Antius inclined his head, grateful for the compliment. Cassius exchanged a quick glance with Anna before speaking up.

"Father," he began. "Are you certain this is a good idea?"

"What?" Claudius said. He was wearing his painting tunic again, as he usually did while working.

"Well, the earthquakes. What if there are more? Do you think it is a good idea to begin if you will be interrupted again?"

"Of course, Son. We cannot live our lives as though lightening will strike us down. That is madness." Claudius was mixing colors together. He was about to start painting on a small section of the wall where Antius had applied a layer of fresh plaster.

"Yes but," Cassius insisted, "this is different." He paused to think of an analogy that would make sense. "Like a storm," he said.

"A storm," Claudius repeated as he experimented with the colors on a plank of wood that had been painted white earlier.

"Yes," Cassius continued. "If a storm is coming, if you *know* it is coming, and there are signs–the winds are blowing, the rains begin to fall–you plan accordingly, right? I mean, you would not go out in the storm. You would stop your work and wait until it is safe. Right Father?"

"Well of course," Claudius said, "even the animals know when a storm is coming. They can smell it, you know," he turned to face Cassius and Anna for emphasis, as though he were revealing a great secret. "Imagine that," he went back to his work. "Amazing things, animals are. Creatures of instinct. Sharp instincts. They sense things we do not."

"Speaking of which," Anna piped in, "have any of you noticed that there are no birds here? None. I have not seen or heard any since yesterday at least. Not a single bird was at the forum today. None in the garden either. None by the streets."

"What does that have to do with anything, Anna?" Cassius asked a little impatiently. He felt he had been building up a case to use in swaying his father's opinion. And now Anna was going off track on a tangent that really had nothing to do with anything. At least that is how he saw it. And his father was always veering on tangents. He did not want Anna to get him started on one now. He would be rambling on for hours otherwise. And Cassius would not be able to steer him back to the point of the discussion.

"Everything," Anna narrowed her eyes at him. "It has everything to do with what you are saying at least," she shot him a look that said she was on his side. "I remember seeing plenty of birds in Rulaneum. I saw them our first day here too. But not now. Not since last night's earthquake." She stepped up closer to a large basket on the marble table and picked up one of the brushes, feeling its soft bristles.

"And?" Cassius prodded.

"And like Claudius said, the animals can sense when a storm is coming. Or in this case the earthquakes. And so maybe the birds have left to a safer place." She raised a single eyebrow and squared her shoulders at Cassius.

"Oh," Cassius nodded, feeling a bit foolish. "Yes, very observant of you Anna," he gave her an apologetic smile. "Very good point. And just the one I was making myself."

"Ah," Claudius said with a shake of his head. "So that is what you are up to, Cassius," Claudius chuckled to himself. "All this talk of animals and storms," he put down the brush he was using. "This is really all about the earthquakes, isn't it?"

"Yes Father. I—"

"No. I do not want to hear anything more about them."

"But—"

"I said no," Claudius repeated with a look that brooked no refusal. "Earthquakes are just a part of this region. Some places have snow. Others have very dry weather. And still others get lots and lots of rain," he explained as he turned back to his work. "Pompeii gets earthquakes. That is the nature of the land here. It moves."

"It isn't safe," Anna said in a lower voice. Claudius looked her straight in the eyes but said nothing. He was tamping down his impatience. He picked up a rag and wiped his hands on it, more out of irritation than anything else. Anna had involuntarily stepped a bit closer to Cassius. He was her ally, after all. Then Claudius faced them both before speaking.

"Is anything safe?" He asked, beginning one of his speeches. Cassius took a deep breath as Claudius dove into his monologue. "The nature of this life," Claudius continued, "is one of risk. Each day that we awaken and dress and go out, we take a risk. Every time we step out on the road we take a risk. Every time we eat or drink we take a risk." He looked at them to make sure they were following. Cassius was already bracing himself for one of his father's long lectures. Anna was imagining Claudius giving this speech at the forum. He had the look and voice of those great orators in history.

"Risk," Claudius continued, "is a part of life. They cannot be separated. Because death is a part of life. They are two sides of the same coin. Life and death. Safety and risk. Peace and anxiety. Growth and decay," he waved his hand in a gesture that indicated a continuum with infinite possibilities. "Paradoxes, all of them, but inseparable," he nodded, seeming satisfied with himself. "Yes, inseparable," he repeated. "And we cannot stop living because we live under the shadow of death. Death's shadow is always there, whether or not we see it," he nodded again, wisely. No one replied. What could possibly be said? It was futile. He would have to see for himself, which he would, soon enough.

"So yes," Claudius finished as he picked up his brush and turned to give his attention to the wooden plank that was leaning against a wall next to him, "you are right Anna. It is not safe. But we must make the best of it regardless. Life isn't meant to be safe. And I am not going to pack up my bags and walk out on a very lucrative commission because it isn't safe. My reputation is at stake. And if I were to leave, I would not get any more commissions. Without commissions my painting career would be over. So if leaving is what you both have in mind, you had better think of something else. We are not going anywhere." And that was that. He dismissed them with a wave of his hand and turned to give his full attention to his work.

"Ah!" He turned back quickly to face them again when he remembered something. "One more thing," he was smiling as though his tirade were already forgotten. "We are dining out tonight. We have been invited by Marcus's friends at their home. Remember? I told you that I may get another commission while we are here. Their names are Gaius and Fabia. It is they who have invited us. So dress accordingly. Only the three of us will be going," he glanced at Antius. "You will remain here Antius."

"Of course," Antius replied.

"Very well then," Claudius said, as he turned back to his work. The waning light that filled the atrium cast shadows on the walls around them. And as Anna watched those shadows move with the motions of Claudius's hand over the wooden panel, she thought of his words and how appropriate they were as they echoed in her mind once again. *We live under the shadow of death,* he had said. Little did he know that this particular shadow was cast by the great primeval mountain that was already awakening from its long and restless slumber.

Chapter 13

The home of Marcus's friends seemed very nice to Anna. It was smaller than the House of the Fountain, and unlike Marcus and his wife, its owners lived there full-time. But Anna could not understand why they wanted to paint anything. Everything looked perfect as it was. The walls in the atrium were decorated with mosaics of mythological scenes that were set within large panels painted deep red and golden ochre, with fantastic architectural elements that framed the art beautifully. Even the floor was a work of art with its limestone tiles framed by mosaics in scrolling patterns that wove through the entire room.

"It is the garden walls that we want redone," Fabia said. She had taken Claudius, Cassius and Anna on a tour of the house.

"Of course," Claudius agreed. "They are peeling from the elements undoubtedly."

"Yes, well," Fabia paused to take a sip from a cup she had been holding, "those walls have not been touched in about fifteen years. Everything else is fairly new. We had them all redone six years ago," she waved her elegant hand about gracefully, encompassing the whole house. "It is truly amazing that they have not been damaged by the earthquakes. But the outside ones are showing tremendous wear. So many cracks," she said with a shake of her head.

Fabia was a sophisticated middle-aged woman with a sense of style that she liked to flaunt in all things from her home décor and dinner parties, to her wardrobe and jewelry. Her husband Gaius was very involved in the political life of Pompeii, and served as one of the magistrates in the legislative body. They often invited friends and associates over their home for dinner parties. Many important ideas and decisions were hatched and honed within the walls of this house. And as the wife of a magistrate, Fabia aimed to exemplify the ideals of Pompeian society as best as she could.

"Marcus has had much work done to the House of the Fountain," Claudius said, "and it shows." They were strolling in the gardens under the columned porch with Cassius and Anna following behind. These gardens were more formally decorated with marble figurines that spouted water into elegant basins. No vines climbed over the pillars or hung from the beams, but the flower beds were divided into neatly manicured sections that reflected an appreciation for symmetry and order. They were lovely in a formal sort of way, inviting one to gaze but not touch.

"It has been a very big project for them," Fabia agreed. "His wife is my sister's niece. They hope to come here more often, especially after the birth of their baby. It is good that they are in Rome while the renovations take place. I do not know how she could live here while work was being done." They had stopped by one of the figurines spouting water. It looked like a garden nymph to Anna.

"Which walls were you thinking of having painted?" Claudius asked her as he looked around the garden.

"The three surrounding the peristyle," Fabia said. "What do you think, Claudius?"

"They could certainly use it," Cassius jumped in with blunt honesty. Claudius shot him a withering glance, but Fabia only laughed.

"You must excuse my son," Claudius began, "he—"

"Oh no," Fabia interrupted Claudius, "I appreciate his honesty very much. It is most refreshing actually," she smiled at Cassius. "It seems that too many people are bent on telling me what they think I want to hear, rather than their true opinions," she shook her head in disapproval. "And that does not help me much at all."

"I am afraid the truth is all you will get with us," Claudius said. They had begun moving back towards the house. Dusk was deepening into night and dinner had been served. "We are not good at dissembling. Neither my son nor me. I am just a painter," he said humbly.

"The best in the region, from what I have heard. Your reputation precedes you, Claudius. Even in Rome they speak of you. And certainly in the best circles. I have heard of your talents and know that your skills are highly regarded," Fabia said emphatically. Claudius inclined his head to her graciously. Anna could see that he was practically glowing with her praise. It might have been her imagination, but he seemed to strut about like a bird that had just been preened.

Anna felt a bit awkward reclining on the couches in the small dining room. It was uncomfortable because they were a larger group of seven people and the space was not ample. They lay close to one another and it was a bit too intimate for

Anna. At least she had been placed next to Cassius, so it wasn't too strange.

Besides the three of them and their hosts, Fabia and Gaius had also invited another couple named Lucius and Sabina. Like Gaius, Lucius was also a magistrate. While Gaius presided over the administration of the judicial system, Lucius was responsible for overseeing Pompeii's public entertainments. He supervised the management of the games in the amphitheater and the shows that were held in the two theaters near the Stabian Gate on the south side of Pompeii.

"You are very welcome to join us tomorrow for the celebration of the Vulcanalia," Lucius said to Claudius. The seven of them were all reclining on the sloping couches that were built right into the wall to save space. The couches were adorned with thick colorful cushions and rich fabrics that draped over the masonry slabs underneath. The walls here were also beautifully painted in architectural motifs that made the room seem larger than it actually was.

"Yes, join us, added Fabia. We are going as well." Slaves brought platters laden with all kinds of savory food. There was stewed rabbit, roasted wild boar, fried fish, boiled goose eggs, baked rounds of dough filled with minced meats and vegetables, dishes of olives, and a variety of cheeses, dates, figs, honey and plenty of flat bread with wine and mulsum to go around.

"Where will it be?" Claudius asked as he reached for one of the eggs. Another slave was filling his cup with wine, then she moved to fill the other cups in the room.

"In the large theater," Fabia said. "It is practically a stone's throw from here." She pointed south, then helped herself to some of the stewed rabbit. At least the theater was closer than the amphitheater, thought Anna. With all the people on the streets, and the animals on parade, it had taken them at least a couple of hours to walk to the amphitheater during the Consualia. The walk back home had not been much better either with all the crowds, many of whom had continued partying well into the late hours of the night.

"That sounds wonderful," Claudius accepted the invitation. "It would be an honor for us to join you."

"The honor is all ours, Claudius, I assure you," Fabia said. "It is not often that we receive so highly acclaimed an artist in our town." With all her compliments, Fabia had Claudius eating out of the palm of her hand. Cassius shook his head at his father and Anna bit back a smile when they saw Claudius's face. He looked very happy and proud as a peacock. If his feathers get puffed up any more, thought Anna, we will not be able to fit him through the door.

"Did you enjoy the festivities and sports in the amphitheater?" Lucius asked. "For the Consualia?" He added, watching Claudius over the rim of his cup of wine. Anna thought that as magistrate of the public entertainments, Lucius probably had a hand in planning the festivities.

"Very much," Claudius answered.

"The sports were phenomenal!" Cassius piped in. He had been riveted at the events in the great stadium, especially the blood sports.

"Spoken like a true fan," Gaius laughed as he bit into some bread.

"And why wouldn't he be?" Fabia said. "The sports were very well orchestrated." Then Fabia turned to Anna, "Did you enjoy it as well Anna?"

"I—" Anna began but was interrupted by Cassius.

"She loved it. Especially the gladiators!" They all laughed at the obvious displeasure on Anna's face. They could see that Cassius was teasing her.

"It is alright Anna," Sabina spoke up kindly. "Even though my husband is in charge of these matters, I do not usually attend."

"You do come, my dear," Lucius contradicted her.

"But only when there are no blood sports," Sabina clarified. "They are just too vicious as far as I am concerned," she said to Anna, as she wrinkled her nose. "It is not suitable for women."

"Speak for yourself, my dear Sabina," Fabia said with a laugh. "I quite enjoy the blood sports."

"That is because you are like a predator, my dear, with a taste for blood," Gaius said as he chuckled. "And you certainly have the heart of a predator."

"Oh really?" Fabia raised a single eyebrow at her husband, but there was no anger there. She knew he was just being playful. But she really did enjoy the sports, even if they were brutal. "I guess I do have a taste for blood," she said with a thoughtful expression.

"It is an acquired taste, I think," Sabina said.

"Oh, I don't know about that," Fabia responded as she sipped a little wine from her cup.

"She has liked the blood sports for as long as I have known her," Gaius said while chewing on a piece of the roasted wild boar.

"In my experience," Lucius cut in as he held a fig in one hand and his cup in another, "one either likes them or dislikes them. There is nothing in between."

"Well you need not worry about seeing any gladiators at the theater, Anna. They only fight in the amphitheater," Sabina told Anna with a comforting smile. "Tomorrow's festivities will be more tame."

"But there will be blood," Lucius added quickly. "It is the Vulcanalia after all."

"How do you celebrate the Vulcanalia?" Anna asked a little cautiously. "Is it like the Consualia?"

"Oh no," Fabia answered. "The Consualia is a much grander festival, as you saw for yourself yesterday. You can see that much of the town is recovering still. In fact," she paused to nibble on a date, "being that both the Consualia and Vulcanalia are so close together, some people leave their shops closed for all three days. They take off from work to celebrate the holidays, almost turning them both into one grand festival." Fabia reached for another date which she ate after sipping some wine.

The food was delicious. Anna made it a point to try everything. She tamped down her natural resistance to avoid eating those things that looked strange to her. Claudius looked very pleased with how the night was unfolding. There was no doubt in Anna's mind that he would get this commission as well. Cassius did not speak as much. He seemed more interested in the food and ate with an appetite suited to an adolescent boy growing by leaps and bounds. Where did all the food go, Anna wondered? He probably burned it off with all his nervous energy.

"As you probably already know," Fabia continued, "Vulcanalia is the feast honoring Vulcan, the god of fire." Anna coughed suddenly as she accidentally swallowed the wrong way. She was stunned by what Fabia had said. Strange how the feast of Vulcan had fallen the day prior to the eruption of the volcano Mount Vesuvius. Could this be a coincidence? It was too uncanny. She was sputtering a little as she caught her breath and tried to keep from choking. Cassius patted her on the back and handed her a napkin.

"Sorry," Anna said as she cleared her throat and settled down with a deep breath.

"Chew carefully, Anna," Sabina told her.

"It was the drink, not the food," Claudius said. Then turning to Anna he said, "Please do be careful Anna."

"I just swallowed the wrong way," Anna blushed and looked away. She felt a little embarrassed.

"It is alright my dear," Fabia told Anna. "All this talk about the festivities has you a bit excited perhaps." Then turning to Claudius, Fabia asked, "Have you been enjoying the sights of Pompeii then?"

"Pompeii is splendid," Claudius replied in his loud voice. "Although I have been mostly inside with my work, Cassius and Anna have spent more time seeing parts of the town," he picked some grapes off a platter brought in by one of the slaves. Then biting into one he said, "But the Consualia was absolutely wonderful. We really enjoyed ourselves yesterday."

"You will like the Vulcanalia too," Fabia said.

"But it is very different from the Consualia." Gaius reached for a fig and held it in his hand as he spoke.

"Much more civilized," Sabina said with a glint in her eyes.

"No human bloodshed, if that is what you mean by civilized," Gaius replied, sinking his teeth into the juicy fruit.

"Perhaps not human," Fabia spoke up, "but there will be plenty of bonfires with animal sacrifices."

Anna winced. That was not something she wanted to see. She remembered learning about how ancient cultures would offer animal sacrifices in order to appease their gods.

"What sort of animals?" Anna asked in a voice that sounded a bit squeaky to her ears. Cassius snickered next to her. He could tell she was uncomfortable with the subject, and it made him laugh to see Anna squirm. Anna narrowed her eyes at him in a warning.

"Small animals," Fabia said as she nibbled on a fig. "Fish mostly."

Anna slumped a bit on the couch.

"Rabbits too," Cassius added with a mischievous grin. He was enjoying Anna's discomfort. She nudged him hard with her elbow.

"There will be plays too," Sabina changed the subject brightly, "and plenty of musicians." She saw that the topic of sacrifices disturbed Anna.

"The plays are my favorite," Claudius said over the rim of his cup. "The masks are fantastic. The comedies–and the farces especially–are hilarious."

Anna could understand how Claudius would have a special appreciation for the plays and their elaborate masks and costumes. It was the artist in him that had an eye for such things. The absurdity of the plots with their cases of mistaken identity and nonsensical humor was very appealing.

Suddenly the platter on the small table between them began to rattle. At first Anna thought that someone was rapping their fingers on its edge. But then the whole house shook from the tremor. Anna sat upright at once, poised to bolt outside. Cassius sat up as well, without any trace of the grin that was on his face a moment before.

"Earthquake Father!" Cassius was as wide-eyed as Anna. His body tightened with fear. Anna felt herself gripping the edge of one of the cushions. Claudius looked a bit disturbed, but not enough to sit up.

"It is nothing," Fabia waved it away with her hand. "See? It is over already." And just to demonstrate her indifference, she picked at a grape and chewed it with a show of nonchalance. The others did not seem disturbed either. "Pompeii is always rumbling," she continued as though bored with the subject. "It is just the nature of the land here."

"That is what I was saying the other day," Claudius added.

"It is *dangerous,*" Cassius said, drawing out the word for emphasis. He stood up from the couch, his eyes bright and blinking rapidly.

"Sit down Cassius," Claudius deepened his tone, his nostrils flared. He schooled his face into a deliberately bland expression, but a vein in his neck was twitching.

"It *is* dangerous," Anna stood up by Cassius in a show of support. "Can't you see how the tremors have been more frequent?" Her voice sounded a bit shrill. Time was ticking. Only two days until Mount Vesuvius was due to erupt. Two days!

"Sit *down,*" Claudius repeated through clenched teeth. He was not about to allow Cassius and Anna to embarrass him. Not here and not now.

"But Father—"

"Now—"

"Wait," Anna shook her head as she deliberately kept from making eye contact with Claudius. She knew he was furious. She focused on the others instead. They continued reclining on the couch as though nothing had happened. But their interest was piqued by the strange outbursts and behavior of Cassius and Anna. They watched quietly now, their heads tilted and eyebrows raised in expectation.

"It is not safe." Anna began rubbing her upper arm in an unconscious attempt to relieve her building anxiety. Claudius sat up but Sabina placed a hand on his shoulder to calm him.

"Let her speak," she said softly. "It is alright Claudius. Let her speak." Sabina turned her gaze back to Anna. Claudius closed his eyes briefly as he tried to regain his composure.

"Think about it," Anna continued, feeling a little braver now that Sabina had intervened. "All those tremors. Something is going to happen. Something terrible," she began to pace. Cassius stepped to one side to give her room. He just watched her intently. "Remember that big earthquake in 63?"

"How can *you* remember—" Gaius began, but Fabia stopped him.

"Remember how there were warning signs beforehand? Lots of tremors?" Anna asked them.

"Yes," Fabia answered in a quiet voice. "There were warning signs. But it has always been this way in Pompeii, Anna."

"No," Anna shook her head. How could she tell them about the volcano? They would laugh at her. They would think she was absolutely mad. How could she tell these people–they, who were learned and cultured and worldly, they who were part of the elite upper classes–the ruling class of Pompeii–and who moved in leading circles with other political elite in the upper echelons of society. How?

They stared at her now, waiting. Waiting for her to speak her mind. They stared. Some regarded her with curiosity as though she suddenly sprouted rabbit ears on top of her head. Others looked at her with sympathy. And others, like Claudius… *no no no*… Anna kept her gaze focused, but not on Claudius. She would just have to deal with him later. Poor Cassius would too.

"No," she repeated, wringing her hands. She shook her head again and looked away. "Hasn't it been years since you have felt any earthquakes here?" Several people had said so, Anna recalled. Didius, and that old woman at the bar in the forum. Anna looked at the small group with wide eyes.

"Yes, it has actually." It was Sabina who answered. Fabia nodded in agreement. Then a thought occurred to Anna.

"Do you have dogs?" Anna asked Fabia.

"Yes…" Fabia answered in confusion. The sudden change of subject threw her off. "We have one dog. But we have not seen him in two days."

"He's missing?" Anna brightened, hoping her theory was correct.

"Yes, actually, he is."

"And when did he go missing?" Anna pressed on. "Was it before or after the earthquakes?"

"After." It was Gaius who answered. He looked a little bored. Bored and irritated.

"Don't you see?" Anna said. "Your dog ran away because he is afraid. He knows something bad is going to happen. He can sense it. Animals can sense things," she said. "And so he ran away to be safe. He went somewhere safer," she nodded to them, hoping they understood. Claudius just closed his eyes for a moment in a grave attempt to control his temper.

"And what does that—" Lucius began, but Sabina cut him off with a hand on his arm.

"Go on Anna," Sabina said. Anna could see the sympathy in her eyes. Or was it just pity?

"These tremors are... they are a warning. The whole town," Anna paused, shaking her head, "No. The whole *region* will be destroyed. Pompeii, Herculaneum, Oplontis, Stabiae, and others... all gone."

"By earthquakes?" Gaius snorted loudly. His eyes mocked Anna. He held the cup in his hand with a clenched fist. And his mouth was pinched, the corners turned down. Lucius had that same look. He rolled his eyes as though he'd had enough of this farce. Claudius's face was red. And seeing the other men's expressions only angered him more.

"That's enough," Claudius stood up, squaring his shoulders against the shame that flooded his veins. Anna made to say something more but Claudius silenced her with a withering glance. "Enough, I said!" He thundered.

Nothing more was said on the subject, but the night had been spoiled. Although the subject was changed and every effort was made to reclaim the levity from earlier in the evening, it was gone. Anna and Cassius were quiet now. They knew they were in for a lecture. And the laughter and joking between Claudius and the others was obviously strained. Yes, thought Anna with a heavy grimness that made her sigh, the night had been ruined. It was far beyond salvageable. Who knows if Claudius would even get the commission now? But does it really matter, Anna asked herself as she remembered the sleeping giant that would awaken the day after tomorrow. Does it *really* matter? And she answered her own question with a shake of her head and a deep sadness. Nothing matters now. Nothing, but escape.

Chapter 14

Nothing was said on the way home. Claudius kept his mouth shut. He did not even glance at Cassius or Anna. But his face was still red. It seemed to grow redder as they approached the House of the Fountain. His body was tense and his jaw clenched. And that vein on his throat pulsated. For a moment Anna was worried that he might have a heart attack or a stroke. He was that angry. Furious.

Anna made to go to her room as soon as they arrived at the house. She wanted to get away and put as much distance as possible between her and Claudius. She hoped Cassius would do the same.

"The strap," Claudius said to Cassius in a controlled tone. "Get me the leather strap, Cassius." Cassius froze in his tracks, his face turning ashen. "And Anna, you are to stay here. You will see what happens to those who are insolent."

Anna did not know what to expect. The strap? But it did not sound good. She watched Cassius as he forced himself to move towards the garden where more of Claudius's supplies were kept. Claudius waited patiently, keeping his eyes fixed on the lattice doors where Cassius had gone. But Anna sensed his anger. It came off him like steam rising from boiling water.

Cassius returned with something in his hand. He walked slowly, hesitantly, towards his father.

"Father—"

"Shut up!" Claudius silenced him. "Not a word. Not a single word." Claudius grabbed the strap from Cassius and uncoiled it. It looked like a long leather belt. "Come to the wall," he demanded. "Turn around. Hands above you with your palms on the wall. Now remove your tunic." Claudius had doubled up the strap so that it formed a wicked loop with the ends secure in his hand. Cassius turned and glanced at Anna. He felt totally humiliated. He did not want her to watch. He was much more afraid of her witnessing this than he was of the punishment itself.

"The tunic!" Claudius shouted. Cassius shut his eyes and tried to control his breathing. His heart was racing, as was Anna's. She turned away, not wanting to see him.

"Eyes here, Anna," Claudius said. His back was straight and he held his head high as he spoke.

Cassius removed the tunic and left it on the floor. He turned to face the wall, placing his hands above as told, with just his undergarments on. He felt small. Anna's heart went out to him. But what could she do? If she were to interfere, Claudius might use that strap on her. And so she held her breath when the beating commenced.

It was over very quickly. Claudius believed in mitigating one's punishment swiftly. He used the strap to whip Cassius rapidly in succession across his back just a few times. And although the sound of the strap cracked loudly as it hit Cassius, stinging where it fell, it did not mark him other than reddening the skin. It sounded worse than it felt. Claudius was a very strong man, but he was also very controlled. He wished to teach his son a lesson, not hurt or scar him for life.

Cassius slumped a little from the fear of the ordeal. He bent down to pick up his tunic and pull it over his head once again, drawing it down to cover his body, like the fabric of his dignity that had been stripped from him only moments before. He kept his eyes down, avoiding Anna's gaze, but Anna saw his eyes shine with unshed tears. He was trying to be brave.

Claudius folded the strap and handed it back to Cassius to return to its place. When Cassius returned, Claudius made to speak but closed his eyes instead. He was trying to compose the thoughts that arose from the turmoil seething within him.

"Tonight," he began, wanting to say much but not sure where to begin. "Tonight was abominable. Abominable!" He caught himself and tried to restrain the anger. "Do you remember earlier today when I said that I do not want to hear anything more about the earthquakes?" He raised his eyebrows as he gave Cassius and Anna a hard stare. "Did you think I did not mean it?" He began pacing about the room as he continued. "You knew–you both knew very well–that this dinner was important to me. Very important. I had told you that they are friends of Marcus and that they are considering commissioning me to paint for them. You knew this. And yet you chose to ignore that and go on speaking your minds like unruly little children who disobey their parents," he narrowed his eyes.

Cassius and Anna had moved closer together. They were standing by the dry shallow pool that sat in the atrium below the open roof. Anna was picking at her fingers nervously, her gaze locked on Claudius. Cassius just stood still.

"Do you think they will want to hire me now? People only hire people they respect. How can they respect a man who is not respected by his own son? And by his son's friend?

How?" He glanced away a moment. Moonlight was spilling into the atrium from the opening in the roof. It cast a bluish haze that made everything seem to glow amid the shadows. But those shadows were cold. They made Anna shudder, and she wrapped her arms protectively around herself now.

"But that is not the worst of it," Claudius continued. "People talk. That is how word gets around. That is how reputations are built. It is also how, with a quick lash of the tongue, good reputations are destroyed," he paused a moment for this to sink in. "Is that what you want, Cassius? To see your father's good name–our family's good name–smeared like the droppings of the animals on the cobbled stones of the streets?" He took a deep breath and let it out slowly. "A reputation, once lost, is lost forever. It cannot be rebuilt. A crumbled reputation is scattered like the stones of a ruin. And if that were to happen," he wagged a finger at Cassius, "it would be on your head, Son."

Claudius then turned to Anna. "This is all your fault, you know. Do you not think that I know that this is your fault, Anna?" He nodded slowly as he continued. "Yes. Your fault. My son would never have done what he did or said what he said if it had not been for you," he pointed a stabbing finger at Anna. "You!" He boomed. "Your influence. You have been filling his head with all this nonsense about the earthquakes and danger. I never should have allowed you to come. What was I thinking?" He shook his head, silently berating himself. "I was too quick to agree." Anna cringed with guilt. She felt herself shrink smaller and smaller. She wanted to go hide somewhere where no one would find her.

"But not anymore," Claudius continued. "No more of this nonsense. No more roaming around freely and doing as you both wish, or saying whatever pleases you. No more," he stopped to think a moment as an idea came to him. His eyes were moving around the room as the idea took form and shape in his head. "There are going to be some changes around here. Big changes. I still have much work to do before we can quit Pompeii and return home. And I am hoping, by some miraculous will of the gods, that maybe Fabia and Gaius will still give me the commission to paint their garden walls. But that all depends on what happens from now on. I cannot have you both running about on the loose. That is too dangerous for my reputation. No. As of right now, you are no longer free. You will both be locked up here until all my work is completed. If I require any supplies or errands, I will send Antius or Didius," he shook his head again, scolding himself for not having done this before. But how could he have known that his own son and Anna would prove to be such a nuisance? More than a nuisance, he thought. A threat to his reputation and livelihood. "Neither of you will leave the walls of this house. And tomorrow, I am going to the theater without you. I am assuming–hopefully–that their invitation to celebrate the Vulcanalia still stands. I will celebrate it with them. But you will stay here. Locked up."

Then Claudius turned towards the lattice doors that led to the slave quarters at the rear of the house. "Didius!" He called. It did not take long for Didius to appear. Not only was his room close by, but he probably heard everything that had happened. Nevertheless he was discreet enough not to glance at Cassius or Anna. He kept his unreadable expression fixed on Claudius.

"Ah, Didius. Good. I am glad to see you. Neither Cassius nor Anna are to leave the house. They are not to step out of these walls, not even in the garden. In fact, I want them each locked up in separate rooms. They are to be watched at all times. Is that clear?" Claudius waited for Didius to respond.

"It is clear, Sir."

"Do their rooms have locks? I want them locked from the outside," Claudius had stepped over to Anna's room and was inspecting the door.

"They can be fitted each with a bar and bolted into place. There will be no possible escape then," Didius said with an even voice.

Anna and Cassius exchanged panicked glances. There was no way that she would allow herself to be locked inside that room, Anna thought. There were less than two days before the eruption of Mount Vesuvius. And if Claudius refused to leave, she and Cassius would leave without him. They would save themselves at least. Anna stepped back slowly as Claudius gave Didius instructions. Cassius didn't move. He was too sore and too tired. But Anna continued moving towards the entrance of the house and the door that opened onto the street. She wanted to bolt. And as Claudius was fiddling with her door in the shadows, and formulating his plans, Anna ran. But not fast enough. Didius, who seemed not to even be aware of her presence in the room, saw her furtive movements. He knew she wanted to flee. He could sense her, poised to run, like a predator senses his prey. And he caught up with her in a few easy strides, grabbing her by the arms. Anna fought him, kicking and screaming, but his grip only tightened.

"Let her go!" Cassius yelled. "Father, have Didius let her go!" Cassius had gone to stand by Anna. He felt helpless. Didius was taller and stronger.

"Oh no you don't," Claudius told Anna angrily. Didius had pulled her back inside the atrium and Claudius moved towards them now. "You have given me enough trouble," he furrowed his brows, jabbing the air with a finger that he pointed at Anna. "Put her in the room," he ordered Didius.

"I want to go home!" Anna screamed. "Let me go, let me go!" She wriggled in vain. Didius pulled her by the arm inside her room, then let her go and closed the door.

"He as well," Claudius ordered, pointing to Cassius. "But in a room upstairs, not down here. I do not want them communicating."

"I can walk on my own," Cassius said as he held up his arms in surrender. He was in too much pain to be touched, and running was not an option. Didius just followed him up the stairs.

Anna was pacing in the room. Her mind was racing all over the place. She glanced at the room's tiny window. It had been cut high into the wall as a precaution against thieves. Yet it also prevented her escape. How would she get out of here? She stepped quietly to the door, leaning her ear against it. Nothing. It was quiet. Claudius must have gone to bed already. Now that he had spent his fury, he must have gone to sleep.

Then a thought occurred to Anna. Maybe Claudius would let them go in the morning. Of course! He must let them go. It had been a long day and an even longer night, after all. He was tired. And his temper got out of control. People sometimes behave impulsively when they are angry. They do and say things they later regret. Claudius would certainly change his mind in the morning. Even if he celebrated the Vulcanalia without her and Cassius. All she wanted now was to be free. She wanted to get out of the room so she and Cassius could leave Pompeii and return to Rulaneum. She wanted to get out of this place before the inferno was unleashed. And with the morning's light Claudius was bound to be more reasonable. He had to be.

Feeling a little more hopeful Anna stopped her pacing and went to sit down on the bed. Then she took a deep breath and let it out slowly. Of course he would be more reasonable in the morning, she convinced herself. She lay back on the pillow. Her eyes were drawn to the window high above her, where the moon's dim light stole through its opening. And staring at the shadows that settled around her bed, her lids grew heavy and she finally succumbed to sleep.

Chapter 15

Voices from the atrium woke Anna. She also heard the clicking and scraping of sandaled feet on the stone floor, as well as movement and various other noises throughout the house. She blinked her eyes in an attempt to throw off the last vestiges of sleep. What time was it, she wondered? How she wished she could peek out the window. But it was light outside, that much she could see. And the sun had already risen because one of its thick rays slanted in through the window and down a wall in the room.

Anna sat up in bed, looking around her. She had fallen asleep in the same tunic she had been wearing last night. At least she had removed her sandals. She must have kicked them off during the night because they lay haphazardly on the floor now. She slipped them on her feet and walked to the door, placing her hand on the lever. Then ever so slowly she tried pushing the lever down. Nothing happened. The door was still locked!

"Hello?" She pulled on the lever. "Hello? Claudius? Didius? Cassius?" She banged on the door with the heel of her palm. "Someone? Please … " Anna leaned her forehead on the door. "Please open the door. Please…" She closed her eyes and stayed there without moving, not knowing what to do. Her thoughts climbed up the stairs to where Cassius had been taken. Was he still locked up in the room as well? Was he even still in the house? What if they had all gone and left her behind? No. She had to stop herself from panicking. She needed to control her thoughts and not let herself get swept away by her wild imagination. She had to be reasonable. She stepped away from the door and sat on the bed with a thump, sagging into the mattress. How she had been hoping that Claudius would come to his senses and let her go. She had convinced herself that he would snap out of his irrational behavior. Anna sighed. It was useless. Time was ticking. And things looked bleaker with every moment that passed.

Upstairs Cassius was sitting on a short stool, staring at the wall with his brows furrowed. He had been pacing earlier, but finally sat down. He thought about Anna, wondering how she was doing. He had heard her voice a while ago. She had been calling out for someone to open the door. But now she was quiet. She must have given up for the moment. He could almost imagine her sitting on the bed, fidgeting with worry. He exhaled some of the pent up frustration that tightened his chest. Then he rubbed his hand along his jaw. It ached. Probably from the tension he felt. He stood up suddenly, accidentally tipping over the stool. He stretched his arms behind him with his hands clasped, then let them fall to his sides. He walked over to the bed and sat down again, running his hand through his hair.

Cassius felt guilty. His thoughts replayed last night's dinner and the scene he and Anna had made. Anna never would have stood up and said anything if he had not done so first. He was the one who got her started on her outburst. If he had just sat down when his father had told him to, neither of them would be locked up right now. But no, he just had to tell everyone how dangerous it was. And what did he really know about it anyway? He was just taking Anna's word for it. No one else seemed to care. They even looked bored by the subject. It was just another tremor after all. And tremors were to Pompeii as currents were to the sea. They just went hand in hand. Could Anna really be right? What if she *was* mad? Now that he thought of it, she really could be mad. Maybe that was why she ran away from home. *If* she really ran away.

Cassius shook his head. He didn't know what to believe. He was starting to feel a little insane himself. All these thoughts ran through his mind like a maze of intersecting roadways crossing over, under, and around each other, but getting nowhere. He could not stop rehashing the events of the previous night. He felt himself clenching his jaw again. No wonder it hurt. At least his body was less sore. He sighed now, feeling guilty for doubting Anna. Something about her conviction told him she was right. He *did* believe her. But what use was that now? Believing is one thing. Doing something about it is another.

Claudius was in the garden finishing up a light breakfast of flatbread and figs. He washed it down with a cup of mulsum, the sweet watered-down wine and honey mixture. He too had heard Anna's calls. And although it pained him to lock them both up, especially after having to whip his son last night, he just could not take the chance of allowing them to go about the town and freely voice their opinions. They would just rile everyone up. Some people did not need an excuse to lose their head and panic. And he certainly did not want his own son and Anna being the instigators.

Claudius was a well-respected man. He thought about his reputation now. His own father had been a painter before him also. But he had been employed in more menial tasks like the painting of the exterior of houses or insulae in white, or the plain background colors inside public buildings. He had not been an *artist,* just a painter. There was a difference.

It was Claudius's mother who had the talent that she passed on to her son. She loved to sketch and paint, and had refined her skills on parchments and wooden panels when Claudius was a little boy. He would watch his mother's hand move gracefully over a blank surface, transforming it into something alive with color, form, light and shadow. Yes, it was his mother's talent that ran through his veins. His humble beginnings in life had been catapulted into the higher ranks of society by that talent. And combined with his father's strong work ethic, Claudius's reputation had taken off far and away beyond his imagination.

But reputations could be fragile things. They had to be nurtured and protected like a delicate creature. After all, the world was full of jealousy, envy and spite. One wrong move could shatter that reputation. And Claudius did not wish for anything to besmirch his good name, least of all the antics or offenses of his own son.

Claudius reran the events of last night as an observer watching a play. He tried to distance himself from the emotions so that he could see things with more clarity and an unbiased perspective. Fabia and Sabina had seemed to enjoy his company–at least *before* the scandal broke. Claudius shook his head slowly, trying not to let his anger rise again. Lucius and Gaius were polite too, even if their behavior was more distant and scripted in the formal and seemingly magnanimous way of politicians. Perhaps they would overlook lasts night's transgressions. Maybe they would even dismiss the whole episode with a casual wave of their superior hands, attributing it to youthful imaginings gone wild. After all, children did have a natural inclination for exaggeration. Perhaps they would understand that and think nothing more of it. Earthquakes and tremors can be frightening things, obviously, but even more so for children. Claudius just hoped that they would see it that way.

Nevertheless, Claudius did not wish to take any more chances. Keeping Cassius and Anna close under lock and key would give him the peace of mind he needed to complete his work. They had abused his trust and the freedom he had allowed them. And now they would remain behind closed doors, out of the way and out of trouble.

Claudius sat back in the chair under the peristyle of the garden. It was overgrown with bushes, shrubs and vines creeping possessively over the columns and beams above. They grew in an unruly tangle that ran wild with an abundance of flowers that vied for the sun's attention. He sipped some of the mulsum as he observed the gardens from the shade. Strange how no birds flew above nor settled in the greenery. All that foliage would make for perfect nesting. It was a bit too quiet. Hmm, he thought, pondering this eerie phenomenon. Anna had been right when she mentioned the absence of birds here. And what about the dog? The mastiff belonging to Marcus? Didius had locked him up to keep him out of Claudius's way. He just couldn't have a large dog running about while he was painting. Perhaps he was still locked away, he thought. He made a mental note to ask Didius about him later. Then he shook his head, brushing aside the doubts that had been planted by

Anna and Cassius. He refused to give in to the suspicions that ruled their minds. No. He was a rational man, not given to worrying about inconsequential things that meant nothing. And dogs or no dogs, he had a job to do. But not today. It was the Vulcanalia, after all. In a while he would dress and meet his hosts at the large theater that awaited, where he would pass the day losing himself in the festivities of the great feast.

Chapter 16

Anna must have fallen asleep. She had been lying down on the bed, staring up at the wall where the sun's light cast strange patterns across its surface. The last thing she remembered was silently tracing those patterns with her eyes when the warmth of the room lulled her into a drowsy slumber. Still lying with her head on the pillow, she turned to face the door now. The only table in the room held a plate of food and a cup of mulsum. Someone must have left it there for her while she was asleep. She sat up, her stomach growling in anticipation. She had not eaten anything since last night at the home of Fabia and Gaius.

The food looked delicious. The flat bread was still a little warm, and there was a dish with cheese and olives. She ate every bite hungrily, then drank the mulsum and left the cup on the table with the rest of the things. She got up to stretch and walk around the room, trying the door's lever once again. It was still locked. What time was it, she wondered? Had Claudius already left the house to celebrate the Vulcanalia? Anna could smell traces of smoke that drifted in through the high window. Not much of a breeze was blowing that she could feel in the small room, but she did smell the smoke of the bonfires outside.

Fabia had told them how during the Vulcanalia many bonfires were lit throughout the town, not only at the theater where a particularly huge pyre would burn honoring the god

Vulcan, but everywhere in Pompeii. People would offer their sacrifices in the open streets where small animals–fish mostly–would be cast into the flames. Anna smelled them now. A small part of her was glad to be locked up in this room away from the blazes. She was not particularly fond of such things, and had no desire to witness them. She walked over to the door now.

"Cassius?" She waited, holding her breath and listening intently. "Cassius!" She called out louder. "Can you hear me? CASSIUS! Cassius! Cassius?" She slumped against the door. Was anybody home?

"Anna?" Cassius had heard Anna yelling his name. "ANNA!"

"YES! I CAN HEAR YOU!" she shouted through the crevice where the door met the frame of the wall. Her heart leaped! Cassius was home too! Still locked away, though. She shook her head. Now what?

"ARE YOU ALRIGHT?" Cassius called out. He was bent down and shouting under the small space beneath the door.

"YES," she answered. At least that was something. At least they could communicate a little. She felt better knowing he was here too. She was not alone. But then she heard footsteps. They approached her room with purpose and determination, and fear bloomed in her chest as she backed away from the door quickly. There was nowhere for her to go. The footsteps stopped. They stopped right outside her door. She listened. Whoever was there was listening also. Anna could feel the beating of her own heart as she tried to control her breathing.

"Who's there?" She asked, trying to sound brave. No response. Her eyes traveled down to where the door hung just above the floor. In the space between them she saw a shadow. Someone was indeed there. Whoever it was just waited. Anna's eyes darted around the room. What should she do?

"Who's there!" She shouted this time. This felt like a game of cat and mouse, and she did not want to be anybody's prey. A noise sounded as something that had been attached to the door was removed. It was probably the wooden bar that had been placed as an extra security measure to block her escape. Then Anna's eyes jumped up to the door lever. Someone was pushing down on it slowly. Her heart beat even faster. She gasped as she bumped into the bed behind her while backing away. Then the door opened. Anna stared silently as a child about eight or nine years old stared right back at her with big brown eyes. He was barefoot in his short tunic that stopped above the knee, and he regarded her with great curiosity as one might look at a mythical creature that exists solely in fairy tales.

Anna let out her breath slowly. She had been holding it unconsciously, bracing herself for the worst. "Hello," she said. He just looked at her, his hand resting on the door lever. Anna stepped closer. She moved slowly so as not to frighten the boy. Now that the door was open, she did not want him to close it again. She wondered if anyone else were home. If anyone was indeed home, she did not want them to find out that he had just opened her door. Better not to ask. Not yet, anyway. Anna walked to the door and the boy stepped aside, still watching her.

"Hello," he replied. They both turned their heads to listen as they heard movement in a room beyond the lattice doors. The boy looked back at Anna with a shy smile. She smiled back, then held her finger up to her lips, asking him to be quiet.

Anna stuck her head out of the doorway, peeking into the atrium. The coast was clear. "Do you know if anyone is home?" She whispered.

"Only Mother and Porcia," he replied, instinctively whispering back to her.

"Gallipor!" A woman shouted. "Gallipor, come here!"

"I must go now," the boy said, "my mother is calling," and he left in a hurry through the lattice doors.

Anna's mind was working quickly. She had no time to waste. Maybe everyone else had left the house. She hoped the boy would not give her away. She really hoped he would not tell anyone that he had let her out of the room. Just as she stepped into the Atrium she heard a noise. It sounded like a key turning a lock. It was coming from the front door! Anna quickly stepped back in her room, grabbing the bar that had secured her door to hide it from whoever was entering. Then she pulled the door shut quietly. Hopefully whoever it was would not notice that her door had been unlocked. Maybe they would just keep walking by. She waited, feeling her adrenaline spike. Her stomach was in knots, and the food that she had eaten earlier sat in her belly like rocks.

Anna heard the shuffling of feet as the front door was opened. She did not move a muscle as footsteps passed by her room. They paused for a moment, but only briefly before continuing on through what Anna guessed was the lattice doors. Maybe it was one of the female slaves the boy had mentioned. What was the boy's name? It had sounded like Gallipor. At least that was what the woman had called out.

Then Anna heard a man's voice coming from deeper within the house. Her heart sank as she recognized its owner. It was Didius. He was the one who had just returned home. Oh no, she thought as she ran a tense hand through her long hair. It hung in a tangled mess down her back. She had not even bothered to brush it or pull it up and out of her face. Her eyes moved randomly around the floor as she tried to think of what to do. She could not stay here. That was too dangerous. Sooner or later they would find out that her door was no longer locked. She could not run upstairs to Cassius. That was too risky. They would only catch her and then who knows what would happen? She certainly did not want Cassius to get whipped again.

What about leaving? She sighed, realizing that was her only recourse. She had to leave the house. But where would she go? She guessed it really did not matter, so long as she was free. Free to come back and help Cassius escape, that is. She could not leave without him. She *would* not leave without him. He had stood up for her and had been punished for it. And even with the beating he never denounced her. He stood by her side at his own risk. She would do no less for him now. He was her friend. She would not leave him here to die tomorrow. Because tomorrow Mount Vesuvius would blow. Time had just about run out. It would be tomorrow. Tomorrow...

Chapter 17

Anna waited until the voices from the rear of the house fell silent. From behind her closed door they sounded like mumbling in the distance. She could just picture Didius standing there beyond the lattice doors looking down with that unsettling gaze of his as he spoke. He had seemed nice enough when they had all gone to the amphitheater for the Consualia. He knew she found the blood sports very disturbing and he had said that he did as well. He just seemed kind and sympathetic. Had it just been an act? She felt like a fool for trusting him. At least now she knew where his allegiance lay. And it certainly was not with her.

Anna opened the door a crack and peeked outside. No one was in the atrium. She stepped out of her room and closed the door quietly behind her so that no one would know she was gone. At least it would buy her enough time to get away, she hoped. It was quiet in the large reception room. The afternoon sunlight poured in through the opening in the roof, filling the rectangular basin below with a pool of light.

She was halfway through the atrium and well on her way to the front door beyond the entrance when she turned to glance behind her. In her anxious state she did not see the painting supplies that had been left on the floor by the wall. And as she turned back around she accidentally stepped on the rim of an earthenware pot, tipping it over with a low thump. Although the pot did not break, the brushes inside rattled loudly enough as they spilled and scattered onto the stone floor. Anna stopped. For an excruciating moment she felt immobilized by fear and uncertainty. Did anyone hear it? She did not wait to find out, but ran for the door instead.

Didius had just finished giving the women in the kitchen instructions when he heard a noise coming from the atrium. It sounded as though one of Claudius's supply pots that held his brushes had tipped or fallen over. He frowned, instantly alert, straightening to his full height and setting his jaw. Claudius was not home and wasn't expected back until later that night. Someone had escaped.

Anna was fumbling with the door and the strange locking mechanism that kept it bolted when she heard footsteps approaching. The adrenaline in her blood made her hands tremble as she began to panic. Just as she glimpsed Didius catching up to her with his long self-assured stride, she managed to open the heavy double doors that gave to the street. And without looking behind her, she took off.

Anna ran out into the street, skirting around the people that were on the sidewalk or walking in groups in the middle of the road. The stones were uneven in parts and she nearly tripped, but then kept pushing herself forward, putting as much possible distance as she could between her and the House of the Fountain.

People were laughing around her. Some of them were carrying wines skins which they sipped and passed to their friends. They were celebrating the Vulcanalia. She peeked behind her but Didius was not there. Perhaps he did not even bother to chase after her. Slowing down now that she felt safer, she tried to calm herself and steady her breathing. "He's not following me," she whispered aloud in an attempt to convince herself that she was safe. Then she draped the thin white linen stole over her head and around her shoulders that she had taken with her. This should help hide her from unfriendly eyes.

Anna passed by one of the bonfires on the street. It burned brightly as more wood was added to keep the fire going and quench the god Vulcan's thirst for destruction. With the harvest now over, all the grain and wheat was especially vulnerable in the summer's heat. People offered sacrifices to Vulcan so that he would avert the hazardous power of the flames from consuming the crops or from burning the town itself. But those sacrifices were in vain. They were futile efforts that fell on the deaf ears of a mythical god whose only power lay in the imaginations of the people who worshiped him. Little did they know that the great volcano's appetite had been piqued so intensely, it was far beyond any human power to appease it. And tomorrow, god or no god, the volcano's fire would scorch and annihilate the entire town and the region surrounding it.

People encircled the blaze now, blithely unaware of the approaching apocalypse, where they sang or chanted as wine flowed freely between them from a large earthenware jug. Every once in a while a small fish was thrown into the fire where it would sizzle and hiss, making the flames jump higher as it devoured the sacrifices in its scorching heat. Smoke filled the air and was carried on the breeze that blew from the west. It mingled with the briny sea air now. The piquant earthiness that ensued was strangely appealing. Perhaps it was its elemental scent that seemed to transport one back in prehistory to a primordial place that silently ran through the people's veins as remnants from the beginnings of time. Anna inhaled deeply of it now as she closed her eyes and allowed herself to be momentarily swept away by the feelings it evoked.

Then someone grabbed her hair. In her reverie, Anna's stole had slipped off her head and hung loosely around her back. She winced as a strong arm grabbed her hair from behind and twisted it once around his wrist, jerking her backwards. Anna screamed. But no one looked her way, and her cries were lost in the noise around her.

"Do not run Anna," Didius said in an even tone that was just above a whisper. "Claudius would be most displeased to find that you were gone. Do you really wish to anger him further?" He turned her around to face him, his hold on her hair loosening slightly as he led her back up the street from where she had come. Anna said nothing. But she was tense with fear and her eyes darted around the street, hoping to find an ally somewhere. Anywhere.

"And what of Cassius?" Didius continued. "How would you feel if Claudius came home and vented his anger on the boy?"

"He won't do that," she replied in a voice that tried to match his even tone. She did not want to show him her fear.

"Really." It was a statement. "And do you really want to find out?" They were walking past the bonfire where the people still celebrated, oblivious to her predicament.

Suddenly Anna kicked Didius as hard as she could, momentarily catching him off guard. His grip on her hair loosened further and she screamed, "Help! Help me! Help me please!" She faced him and pointed as the other people turned to see what the commotion was about. "He's trying to kill me!" She fibbed. But it worked, getting their attention. One man pushed Didius back hard enough so that he hit the bolted shutters of the closed shop behind him. Another one drew a dagger that had been tucked into a scabbard that hung from the belt of his tunic. He held it up against Didius's throat. "Leave the girl alone," he hissed.

"She's my daughter," Didius lied. "And she is trying to run away. I am taking her back home."

The man let go of Didius and stepped back. Anna looked at both of them as she inched farther away.

"No!" She said. "It's not true! He's lying!" But they didn't believe her. They just watched quietly. So she took off.

Anna ran as fast as her sandaled feet could take her. She dropped her stole and kept running, lifting the hem of her tunic so she could widen her stride. Weaving in and out of people, a new rush of adrenaline flowed through her veins. Didius was not that far behind. He had been momentarily stunned when he hit his head hard against the shutters, but he seemed to recover quickly.

Running past a thick group of people that were walking towards her, Anna turned down another street and ducked into a darkened alcove that opened up to an insula. This particular insula was large with two-story houses and many single or double room dwellings that sat above various shops–some of which were presently closed. And as she made her way through the numerous passageways and public spaces that connected the structures, she exited onto another street and found a shop that faced a busy marketplace. She quickly ducked under one of the tables in the shop that was obscured in part by the shadows that concealed it from the street. She hid. And she waited.

Earthquake ... Anna braced herself as another tremor shook Pompeii. She was crouched tightly under the table and against a corner of a wall. She could see the robes and sandaled feet of the people walking by. She waited there, willing her heart to slow its pounding. She forced herself to breathe more slowly so she could calm down. How did she get herself into this mess, she wondered? She needed to free Cassius. She had to find him and help him escape without being caught herself. As another tremor rocked the table above her, an earthen jar crashed to the ground, its jagged shards strewn before her. Anna stared at one of the pieces, its bold red paint the color of blood. She stared and her thoughts roamed back to the gilded mirror. Would she ever see it again?

Chapter 18

Cassius was pacing again in his room. He was glad that Anna had heard him. At least she was safe downstairs, even if she was locked up. He heard some noise a while ago but just assumed it was Didius or the slaves going about their work. The stone house echoed and had a way of amplifying even the smallest sounds. But what Cassius did not know, was that Anna was gone.

When the earthquake hit, Cassius froze. There wasn't anywhere for him to go. He just stood in the middle of his room, watching wide-eyed as things trembled with a life of their own. Not long after that, another tremor shook the house. This time he jumped up on the bed and looked outside the window. Being on the second floor, this window was lower than those on the first floor. There was no danger of thieves scaling the walls and entering the house through this opening. It was too far up for them to climb. He leaned out far enough to catch a partial view of the street around a corner. People did not seem to really notice the earthquakes. Some of them even laughed, tossing their heads back and gulping down more wine from the skins they carried with them.

Cassius looked around the room for the hundredth time. There was nothing he could use to help him escape. His father wasn't home yet, and Didius would just ignore him anyway. He looked out the window again, running a restless hand through his hair. It was too far to jump. And the blankets on his bed were just not long enough to fashion into a rope. Unless... Cassius was thinking, unless he was able to somehow tear the blankets into strips and tie them together. No... he shook his head, pressing his lips together into a hard line. That would not work. He would need to secure one end to something in the room, otherwise he would fall. He looked around the room again as he exhaled loudly from his mouth. There must be a way out of here. There must.

Anna was not sure how long she remained hiding under the table in the marketplace. But she was sure that Didius had not given up. He was not the kind to throw up his hands and walk away in defeat. And so she waited, her gaze fixed on the feet of the people walking by. She knew that she could not sit here forever. Eventually the shop would close. And then what? She would be flushed out of her hiding place like a sparrow. Or else, she would be trapped inside once the shutters had been locked. Neither scenario looked good. She had to think of something else. Another alternative. Something that would throw Didius off her tracks.

Anna peeked from another side of the table, trying to getter a better view of the shop and its contents. Besides some pottery items, there were stolas and cloaks, toy figurines carved out of wood, and several other collectible items. It looked like it could be a souvenir shop. Maybe this was the Roman equivalent of a modern day souvenir shop. And that could be why it was open today.

Anna guessed that she probably was not very far from the theater. Although she did not know exactly where she was, it had to be close to the main town events, because these shops probably catered to those people on their way to or from the festivities. It was certainly a main part of the town, because the crowds were thicker here. It just made sense that the open shops would line the main roads in hopes of snagging some unsuspecting buyers and making a few sales. After all, people usually cast their nets where there are fish. And from what Anna could observe, the fish were in plentiful supply here. At least that made it easier to hide, she thought, as she wrapped her arms around her legs and rested her chin on her knees. She sat watching the street from her secret nook as the crowd flowed like the Sarnus River that moved along its path. It had a calming effect and she soon found herself lulled into a kind of lethargic reverie.

Didius glanced up above from the street where he stood. The shadows had grown longer as the sun followed its ancient course across the sky. It was close to sunset and Claudius would be coming home soon. Coming home to bad news, thought Didius as he clenched his jaw in frustration. He prided himself on his being reliable. He had been working for Marcus as a paid slave for some years. Now that Marcus had risen even higher in his career as a prefect of the Praetorian Guard under the new emperor, Didius's prospects looked far better than before. And he had no intention of allowing this little incident to harm those prospects.

He had seen Anna turn down a street and duck into the opening of an insula. He suspected she would try to lose him in the marketplace that lay beyond that. He was walking there now. Most of the shops were still open, but a few of the shopkeepers had begun to put away their wares and draw the shutters to close them for the night. Didius narrowed his eyes in suspicion. This would be a perfect place for Anna to hide. She probably found temporary refuge in one of these shops. He slowed his pace, scanning them one-by-one as he walked on the paved road.

Some people had entered the shop where Anna hid. They were looking at the figurines on the table that lay on the other side of the shop. She knew that it was probably getting close to closing time, and that she would have to leave soon. She did not want to get into more trouble if the shopkeepers found her and suspected her of being a thief. Maybe Didius had gone back to the house by now. She peeked over at the people by the other table. They were busy haggling with the shopkeeper over some items, and all their backs were turned. Anna scooted out from under the table and exited the shop. She felt achy from crouching there for so long. She could still smell the smoke from the bonfires that burned throughout Pompeii. Where would she go from here, she wondered?

Didius finally spotted Anna. She wove through the crowd slowly as though she were not sure of where she was going. He followed her for a while, wanting her to relax and let her guard down. Claudius would be home soon and Didius needed to be there before that, but *with* Anna. Slowly he closed the distance between them, ducking out of sight whenever she would pause to have a look around. Finally he got close enough to grab her by the arm.

Anna gasped, her face turning white. Didius's grip on her arm was like a vise.

"It is no use running, Anna," he said in a low voice. "Where will you go? At least you will have a roof over your head at the House of the Fountain." Anna just sighed, realizing he was probably right. She just wanted to be close to Cassius so she could help him, or at least make sure he was alright. And running away might only get him into more trouble. "Besides," Didius continued, as he led her down a road that would take them home, "Claudius will come home soon. Do you want me to tell him about your little adventure today?" He cast her a sidelong glance, gauging her reaction. She said nothing, but her face was drawn. She seemed to have grown smaller somehow. "If you behave, I will keep this little escapade a secret. I will not tell him about today." Didius waited for her to respond. Anna finally looked at him and nodded.

"Alright," she said tiredly. "I will not try to run again. You can let go of my arm." She looked down at her arm where his hand was clasped. Didius narrowed his eyes for a moment, trying to determine whether or not he could trust her. Then he let go.

When Claudius returned to the House of the Fountain he was in high spirits. His day at the theater had gone well. He was not even upset when he arrived to see Anna and Cassius together in the dining room.

"Father," Cassius said as Claudius walked in. Cassius sat up immediately. He and Anna were having something to eat.

"Didius let you both out, I see," Claudius lifted an eyebrow at them. "It does not matter now," he waved his hand dismissively. "I got the commission after all," he raised his chin proudly. Cassius was happy for his father. He felt relieved to be out after having spent the day in the room. And he was thankful that his own behavior last night did not hurt his father's prospects. Neither Didius nor Anna mentioned Anna's little exploit to Cassius or anyone else.

"They did not even mention the two of you," Claudius continued as he helped himself to a piece of bread. "I think they were relieved that you did not come." He chewed in silence for a few moments before going on. "No one wants to be around a bearer of ill tidings."

"Did you feel the earthquakes today Father?" Cassius needed to speak about this to his father. Before Claudius had returned, Cassius and Anna had been talking quietly together. Anna had told him how the great mountain was due to erupt tomorrow. She did not know what time it would happen, only that it would be preceded by stronger earthquakes. They would have to leave before that happened, or they would be trapped and die here.

"I do not want to hear a word about that," Claudius frowned. He regarded his son and Anna as he helped himself to a cup of mulsum. Then his expression softened a little. "You are afraid, aren't you?"

"Yes, Father. Very afraid."

"I need to tell you something," Anna spoke up. She too had sat up when Claudius returned. She straightened her back now and looked at him squarely in the eyes, willing him to listen. Claudius inhaled from his nose, then released it slowly from his mouth.

"Very well," he gave in. "Speak. But I do not want to hear of it after this."

"Tomorrow something terrible will happen," Anna began. Claudius started to roll his eyes but Cassius touched him on the arm to get his attention. "The mountain will erupt," Anna could see the confusion in Claudius's eyes. "Like a kind of explosion," she explained. "It will burst from the top and lots of smoke and fire will escape," she did not know how else to explain it, especially to people who had never heard of such a thing. "There will be terrible earthquakes too, much stronger than we have felt so far." Anna paused a moment before continuing. "When that happens all of Pompeii will be destroyed."

"By the mountain," Claudius said in a flat, even voice.

"Yes," Anna replied, "destroyed by the mountain."

"Father," Cassius interjected, "it is true. Everything that Anna has told me so far has happened."

"What do you mean?" Claudius shook his head. He looked annoyed.

"About the birds, about the dog... it is gone, by the way. Didius said he has not seen the dog in a few days. It has left. Probably with other animals from the town too. At least those that have not been tethered or chained."

"Remember how Fabia mentioned that their dog was missing also?" Anna reminded him.

"Yes, but," Claudius waved his hand, "that has nothing to do with anything."

"But it does," Anna insisted. "It has everything to do with what will happen tomorrow." Anna stood up and began to pace a little. "Animals sense things that we do not."

Claudius said nothing. He was remembering how strange it was that there were no birds outside that morning. The gardens here were a sanctuary for birds. He had found it very odd that none, not a single one, was out.

"Father—" Cassius was sitting on the edge of his seat, leaning forward.

"I do not want to hear anymore," Claudius cut him off. "You have had your opportunity to speak."

"One more thing," Anna added. The urgency was evident in her voice. "*Please,*" she insisted, her eyes pleading with Claudius, "and then I will not say anything more."

"Very well," Claudius sat back and crossed his arms over his chest.

"Can you..." she began, unsure of how to phrase her question. "Will you promise me one thing? May I at least ask you to do one thing?"

"What?"

"If... or *when* you see it begin to happen... tomorrow, I mean. When you see what I have told you begin to happen—with the mountain and the earthquakes—will you believe me then? Will you listen and leave Pompeii? Because there will not be any time left once the volcano—" Anna stopped herself to rephrase, remembering that they did not know what a volcano was, "once the mountain blows."

Claudius closed his eyes for a moment as he pondered his answer. Then he nodded, "Very well."

"You will believe me?" Anna asked again in disbelief, feeling hopeful.

"If all that you say really does happen, I would be a fool *not* to believe you."

Anna exhaled as she sat back down next to Cassius. A wave of relief washed over her, and she sagged with the sudden release of tension.

"I am going to bed now," Claudius announced as he stood up. "It has been a long day—a good day of course," he amended, "but a long one nevertheless. Goodnight. Until tomorrow," he told them as he walked out of the room.

Chapter 19

Morning dawned especially bright in Pompeii. The sky stretched in an endless canvas of blue, unmarred by a single cloud. The summer sun bathed the town in a splendid warmth that radiated far beyond its fortified gates, extending over the countryside to the east and the bay on the west, which sparkled like glass, catching the light from the sun. Anna had spent most of the night tossing and turning with anxiety. When she finally fell asleep, it was with a kind of abandonment of one surrendering to death. A knock on her door had awakened her finally. It was Cassius.

"Anna," he said in a low voice as he opened the door and entered the room. "You are still asleep?"

"Not anymore," she replied, stretching on the bed. Then she sat up, her eyes widening with the realization that today was August 24. "Cassius," she looked at him. Then her eyes darted around the floor as her mind began to work.

"Yes. I know," he replied. "But you should look outside. It is beautiful. A perfect day. It's hard to believe anything could possibly happen."

Claudius and Antius were already working in the atrium. Anna could hear movement and their voices carrying.

"Let us go for a walk," Cassius suggested. "I have not left this house in two days."

"But we can't," Anna replied anxiously. "I want to stay close to the house so we can be ready to tell Claudius when it happens. We must stay close, Cass."

"I need to go stretch my legs, Anna. I cannot sit here waiting. I will go mad otherwise. Come. I promise we will not go far. Get ready and I will meet you in the atrium."

They left the House of the Fountain and walked down a street towards the forum. Cassius took some bread and fruit for them to eat as they roamed, and a leather flask of mulsum which he hung across his shoulder from a strap. It felt good to be outside and wander about without running in fear. People were unbolting their shops, lifting the shutters and displaying their wares on tables or hanging them from rods. A baker was removing freshly baked bread from the oven. Fullers were busy cleaning the laundry in their shops. It was just another day in Pompeii, or so it seemed.

Cassius and Anna arrived at the forum and went over to sit at the edge of the fountain that graced the center of its open square. They chatted and ate together, passing the time watching the people go about their work or walking by carrying things to sell or items they just bought. But Anna was tense. She could not smell the sea today. No breeze stirred over the town. It was very still. And the sun that had climbed higher in the heavens now shone brilliantly over everything.

Suddenly a splitting crash thundered over the region as the earth shook violently, shattering the eerie stillness that had reigned only moments before. Anna and Cassius turned at once to face the mountain north of Pompeii. To their horror and fascination, a great greyish column of ash burst forth from the volcano, and began climbing many miles into the air like a thick smoky cloud. They were riveted to the scene as it unfolded in a kind of slow motion that seemed to distort their sense of time.

"It is happening!" Anna screamed, wide-eyed with fear. "Cass! It is happening!" They stood there a few moments longer, paralyzed by uncertainly and dread. It was simply mesmerizing. Curious people around them walked over to get a better look at the mountain that spewed a great pillar from its crater. They had no idea of the danger they were in as they gazed spellbound. But another earthquake, stronger still, tore through Pompeii, jolting some of the people out of their trances. Several columns in the forum toppled over, crashing to the ground. Some people screamed, hurrying to bolt the shutters of their shops and flee, while others simply ran for their lives. And still others watched like statues, seemingly oblivious to what was going on around them, unable to tear their gazes away, totally captivated by Mount Vesuvius.

"It is Vulcan! It is Vulcan!" One man cried as he stared at the volcano.

"No, it is Jupiter!" Another yelled back. "Jupiter has been angered!"

"The gods are enraged!" A woman shrieked, as she ran out of the forum.

"Yes!" Others screamed. "Enraged!" More people panicked and ran, but many more stood and watched in morbid fascination. None of the people had ever seen a volcano. They were completely ignorant of its destructive power.

"Hurry!" Anna pulled Cassius's hand as they fled the forum and ran. "Your father! We must get him and go!"

When they arrived to the House of the Fountain, they found Claudius, Didius and Antius all standing on the balcony upstairs with their gazes fixed on Mount Vesuvius.

"Father!" Cassius yelled from below. He entered the house and mounted the steps two at a time, almost tripping in his haste. Anna was right behind him, lifting the hem of her tunic so she would not fall.

"Have you ever seen such a thing?" Claudius spoke in a daze to no one in particular. The great pillar of pumice that rose from Vesuvius began to spread outward like a mushroom, casting a terrible shadow below its great cloud. A frightful darkness stretched out over the landscape as the cloud expanded like an umbrella. Anna and Cassius could not help staring at the incredible sight before them, along with the other three. It was unreal. Then slowly fine ash began to fall from the sky. Claudius put out his hand, letting them fall in his palm. He squinted his eyes, perplexed, as he smelled the charred bits of crushed cinders. The sudden change in the sky and landscape was mystifying. Strange how it had been so calm just that morning. *The calm before the storm,* thought Anna. Always the calm before the storm.

"We must leave, Claudius! We must leave now!" Anna said, tearing her gaze from the sight.

"Yes, Father!" Cassius yelled. "Everything Anna said is true! It is happening just as she said it would."

"*I* am not going anywhere," Didius stated resolutely. "My duty lies here. I cannot abandon the House of the Fountain," he shook his head. "It is only smoke," he waved his hand dismissively. "It will blow away soon enough. I will not leave this house. Marcus would not have me do so." He stood watching the mountain with his shoulders back, chest thrust out, and chin held high, as though he were challenging the volcano to a duel. Anna just looked at him with a baffled frown.

"Father!" Cassius insisted with fear in his eyes. Claudius stood silently, contemplating the tremendous sight before him. He could not seem to pull away from the balcony. Antius returned inside where he went to begin collecting the supplies of Claudius. Cassius finally grabbed his father's arm and pulled him back inside the house. "Now, Father!" He repeated. Claudius followed Cassius and Anna. He was entranced by what was going on.

"Wait," Claudius said, hesitating. "Perhaps Didius is right," he began, his voice full of doubt. He looked away from Cassius and Anna, towards the open roof of the atrium. Ash was drifting down to the shallow basin. It reminded Anna of snow. A grayish-singed snow. "Perhaps it is nothing more than smoke," Claudius continued. "We will be fine if we stay inside. The winds will carry it away." A breeze had indeed begun to stir, but it blew southeast, right over Pompeii.

"No, Father," Cassius spoke up again. "It is dangerous here. We cannot stay. We must go. Now!"

Slowly the darkness spread as more ash fell over Pompeii. A rotten sulfurous smell filled the air. People held parts of their tunics or cloaks over their faces in a futile attempt to keep from breathing the suffocating stench. Fragments of rock and pumice began to shower over the region. It fell lightly at first, and many people sought shelter from the falling debris inside their homes. But many others ran through the streets in a panic with pillows tied over their heads to protect themselves from the fallout as they fled. Some were convinced that this was somehow due to the wrath of their gods.

Many of the people escaped the town with little else but their lives. Those who headed towards the countryside on the east were trapped as more ash and pumice rained down on them, clogging the roads and blocking the streets. And to the west, the sea now churned and roiled in a sudden violent rage, exposing a desolate shoreline with its stranded heaps of fish, creatures, and the scattered remains of refuse strewn on its shores. And as darkness engulfed the day, blocking out the sun, more pandemonium ensued.

Claudius bent down to collect some of his things, but Anna stopped him.

"No Claudius," she said in a firm tone. "There is no time for that. Leave them. Leave everything. Let's go."

"But I cannot leave my pigments," Claudius snapped in his deep voice. "They are very expensive!"

"Our lives are worth much more than the pigments, Father," Cassius added. "Leave them!"

Cassius led the way to the front door. As soon as they stepped outside they knew they were in trouble.

"Let's grab some pillows!" Anna yelled. She ran back inside and took four large cushions from the couches of the dining room. "Hold them over your heads!" She passed one to Cassius and the other to Claudius. "But wait, where is Antius?"

Cassius ran back inside. "Antius!" He called. Antius pushed into the atrium from the lattice doors. He was holding a large pot of supplies. "Leave that!" Cassius told him. "Hurry! We must go now!"

The four of them turned down one street when Anna stopped them. "No! This way!" She pointed north.

"But that is where Vesuvius lies!" Claudius objected. "We must head south, away from the mountain."

"No!" Anna insisted. "The wind will carry all the ash and rock south. We must head north the same way we arrived here."

"Listen to Anna, Father!" Cassius yelled. People were screaming and running through the streets. "She knows!"

"Fine." Claudius gave in, his jaw clenching. He held the pillow over his head as he followed Cassius, Anna and Antius. They were moving as fast as they could, maneuvering through the streets that were dense with people, carts and debris. The layers of ash and rock were growing thicker on the roads, making it harder for them to move quickly. A donkey was stuck in the middle of the street, hitched to the cart behind it. Its owner had fled, leaving the poor beast to his fate. Anna heard the whining and barking of the dogs that were abandoned, still chained to their posts inside houses. She saw a child, eyes wide with fear, peeking out of a doorway to a house where he sat with his family, waiting in vain for the danger to pass. An old man crouched by a wall under a small portion of roof that extended above him. He had his arms wrapped around a small child who buried her head in his cloak. A woman held a baby wrapped in a linen blanket close to her chest, as she ducked under a wayside shrine. It broke Anna's heart to know that so many would not flee. They would die here. Die in unbearable torment and terror.

They continued moving with their eyes fixed on the road ahead. Anna tried to concentrate on placing one foot in front of the other as her heart pounded in fear. A roof collapsed with a resounding bang as it caved in from the pumice and rock that weighed it down. Another did as well farther down the road. And others still. More screams filled the air as Anna winced. She braced herself against the panic that spiked the adrenaline in her blood. Then the earth shook again, this time even more violently than before, as debris rained down harder on the town.

Cassius, Anna, Claudius and Antius tread steadily through the deepening pile of pumice and rock that clogged the streets. At last they exited through the gate they had entered only days before. It seemed like ages ago to Anna. People everywhere were headed south, as far as possible from Mount Vesuvius. Little did they know they were heading in the wrong direction–right where the greatest damage would occur–in the very path where the eruption and fallout would affect the utmost destruction.

The ash continued to fall, coating the landscape a dingy gray as the sky grew ominously darker. On and on the little group trod, putting greater distance between them and Pompeii. More earthquakes shook the ground as lightening tore through the sky in angry, jagged streaks. They walked with their heads bowed protectively under the cushions, their eyes fixed on the ground as they tried to keep their balance over the rising stratum that fell from the sky. It was a grueling ordeal. But slowly the fallout here seemed less dense as they crossed over the foothills that ran west of Vesuvius. The wind was indeed carrying it south and away from them. And finally, after several intense hours, they arrived to the point where Anna had first spied the Bay of Neapolis when they had crossed over here several days back.

They stopped now, pausing to catch their breaths and turn around to look behind them. Their tunics were torn and filthy. Their faces streaked with sweat, dirt and grime from the ash and their exertions. No one said a word. They all stared, shocked and speechless, at the gathering apocalypse. Claudius's eyes were glazed and hollow as though he had stared Death itself in the face. And he had. Cassius watched by Anna's side, reaching for her hand which she took and squeezed reassuringly. Antius's face was drawn with a single deep line etching his forehead between his brows.

The sea which had shimmered gloriously that first day was now a whipping mass of rough waves, their frothy peaks a greyish-yellow. The sky that stretched resplendent under a dazzling sun just that morning, was now plunged in darkness. They could not even see Pompeii anymore. Only a vague outline of the town was visible now, a smudged and muddled hint of a fast-dying metropolis. Vesuvius roared louder as the voices and screams of the people, and the bawling of the wind that spat rocks below, blended into a chaotic symphony of terror. A malevolent opus of destruction.

It was the end of the world. *This* world, thought Anna, as they turned their backs to the disaster and continued on to Rulaneum, treading on the ancient road that stretched out before them. They did not need the cushions anymore, and left them by the wayside, torn and streaked with dirt and ash. They made their way in a heavy silence that choked away any possibility of conversation. Nothing could be said.

Anna thought of Didius who had insisted on staying back at the house like a guard dog. She thought of the donkey they had passed on the street, trapped by the burden to which he was harnessed, and the dogs chained to their posts. She thought of the people seeking shelter from the fallout in their houses or in alcoves they found along the streets, hoping to ride out the storm until it passed. She thought of the shrieks and wails of those people who ran in a panic, their terror escalating with the wrath of Vesuvius.

It was too overwhelming to comprehend. And as the hours passed and the darkness remained farther behind, she felt her face grow wet from the silent tears that rolled down her cheeks. She wept for the people of Pompeii. She wept for the destruction of their town. She wept for humanity everywhere throughout the ages in the great continuum of time that suffered senseless loss, pain and ruin. And finally, she wept for herself, and her own frailty and insignificance in the grand scheme of it all. She wept…

Chapter 20

By the time they arrived to Rulaneum it was very late at night. Dawn was only a couple hours away. Antonia had received them with many questions, but Claudius just waved them away. He looked like a man defeated in battle. They were a bedraggled group that had just barely escaped death. All Anna wanted now was to collapse on a bed and sleep. Maybe in sleep she could escape the screams that still echoed in her mind.

Morning dawned eerily in Rulaneum. The sun shone through a blurry haze of golden-yellow light that coated the air. It was as though nature everywhere knew of the catastrophe suffered in Pompeii. Even the people of Rulaneum had felt the effects of the great earthquakes that rocked the region. Those earthquakes extended beyond the province that lay by the Bay of Neapolis, gripping the earth like the tentacles of a monstrous fiend whose greed could not be sated. And when Anna and Cassius stood outside and gazed to the south later that day, they could still see the darkness that loomed there, hovering like an ominous cloud.

"How did you know, Anna?" He asked her, their gazes fixed to the south. Anna just shook her head in reply, and Cassius let it go. Claudius had a fitful night and had come down with a fever. He lay in bed inside now, with Antonia caring for him.

A somber mood cloaked the house. Little was said as they all retreated into the confines of their minds, seeking what solace they might find from the terror they had witnessed. Some things are too overwhelming to talk about. They need to be pondered and digested bit by bit first. And even then, there was little that could be said. Sometimes it is best to let sleeping dogs lie, Anna thought. She smiled ruefully to herself as she remembered her grandmother. It was something that Baba said on occasion. After all, there are things in this world that make no sense whatsoever. No rhyme or reason. It is best to let those things go. Yes, thought Anna, Baba was right. But it was far easier said than done.

Anna turned to face Cassius now. They were strolling through the streets of the small town. Everywhere Anna was reminded of Pompeii: a bakery they passed with the smell of fresh bread wafting on the breeze, a bronzesmith with the clanging of metal, a fuller with the washing of clothes. The shops here were open, their shutters up for business. People roamed the streets in pairs or leading mules or donkeys that pulled the carts behind them. Others carried baskets with food, or jugs with wine or oil. They passed different taverns and bars that were tending to the patrons eating there. They passed the wayside shrines and public fountains that shimmered in the pallid light.

"Will you go back home now?" Cassius asked Anna. He was fidgeting with the edge of his belt, and kicking at a small pebble on the street.

"Yes," she replied, keeping her eyes on the pebble. She did not want to cry. Anna sighed and Cassius exhaled a long drawn out breath at the same time. Then they both looked at each other and laughed suddenly.

"What is so funny?" He asked her, a smile playing about his lips.

"Nothing, I guess," she glanced away a moment, watching a woman fill an earthen pitcher with water from a public fountain. "It's just that," she shook her head, "we must look like quite a pitiful pair, sighing at the same time, and forlorn."

"We have reason to be," Cassius replied.

"Do we?" Anna tilted her head, regarding him with a quizzical look. "We made it. We made it out of Pompeii. And just in time too. We survived." She observed a child sitting on a step next to his father's shop. He was playing with a little wooden figurine. "I am grateful," Anna told Cassius. "So grateful, you know."

"For what?" Cassius was also watching the boy play.

"For coming here," Anna answered. "For meeting you, for going to Pompeii, for surviving and coming back. For everything, really," she tucked a loose strand of her hair behind her ear. The little bracelet on her wrist caught the light then.

"You still have it," Cassius said, looking very pleased as he reached for her hand to get a closer look at the bracelet.

"Of course," Anna smiled. "It is very precious to me. I will always treasure it, Cass," she looked down at the bracelet, its delicate silver strand glinting in the sun.

That night Cassius and Anna dined alone with Julia, while Antonia stayed with Claudius by his bedside. Julia was full of questions now that word had begun to spread about the eruption of Mount Vesuvius and the terrible disaster that followed. Her eyes were all aglow and wide with interest and curiosity. Anna was glad she had not been there to experience it. Innocence, once lost, was rarely found again. And there is nothing like tragedy and disaster to crush the innocence of youth.

Anna and Cassius stayed up long into the night chatting and playing games like tic-tac-toe and knucklebones, which was similar to jacks. He knew she would be leaving in the morning. Neither of them wanted to think about that now.

The next day Anna accompanied Antonia and Cassius to see Claudius in his room. He was tucked in bed, looking very somber. His face was still a little flushed from fever, but at least he was not getting any worse. He even claimed to be feeling a little better, but Antonia would not allow him out of bed. Julia had been keeping him company, playing with a doll on the floor.

"Anna," Claudius greeted her as they entered the room.

"Hello Claudius," she gave him a small smile. Claudius tried sitting up, but Antonia would not hear of it. He just sighed as he tried to make himself more comfortable.

"Anna," he began, his voice still strong despite the illness. Even sick he still had a booming voice, thought Anna. "Anna, Anna..." he repeated, shaking his head sorrowfully. "I owe you an apology," he said.

"No—" Anna replied as she held up a hand in denial, but he cut her off.

"Yes. I do. I owe you a thousand apologies," he looked away at the window cut high into the wall. A watery light spilled into the room through its opening. Then he turned back to face her. "A thousand apologies," he repeated, nodding his head gravely. "You..." he began again, but stopped to collect himself. "You saved our lives. And I am so grateful, so *infinitely* grateful... for myself, for my son, for Antius..." he stopped to inhale, then exhaled slowly. "For my wife, my daughter," he continued. "Thank you," he nodded again. "Thank you Anna." Anna did not say anything. She did not really know what to say. She just took his hand and squeezed it gently. Then she leaned down to kiss him on the forehead. He just smiled in that fatherly way of his.

Cassius accompanied Anna as they walked to the forum in Rulaneum. The sky was absolutely breathtaking. A haze of smoky clouds filtered the sun in ethereal colors that were simply stunning. The previous night the sunset had painted the sky in passionate reds and violets. It was due to Vesuvius. The cloud of ash and debris that was catapulted into the air had also smeared it in the most intense colors. Anna wondered at how something so destructive could also be responsible for something so beautiful.

They walked by the busy marketplace with its colonnaded galleries and elegant porticos. Then they arrived to where Anna had bumped into Cassius that first day when she had first come to Rulaneum. She was so glad she did bump into him.

"Do you think we would have met if I had not bumped into you?" She turned and asked him suddenly.

"I do not know. Maybe," he said, a wry smile playing about his lips. "You seem like the kind who is always bumping into trouble," he winked, and they both laughed.

Cassius was carrying an empty basket with him. He was on his way to buy new pigments for his father, since they had to abandon their supplies in Pompeii.

"At least you brought a basket with you this time," Anna teased him. "You don't want someone else bumping into you. Maybe the vials would break this time. You can't push your luck, you know."

"I do know, Anna," he said, suddenly serious. "It was not luck. I do not know what it was, but it was not luck. It was far better than that." He looked away.

"Well, then," Anna said as they stopped walking. They stared at nothing in silence for a few minutes. Then Anna bit her lip and sighed again. She turned to face him then. "I hate saying goodbye, Cass," she looked away, willing herself not to cry.

"Then don't," Cassius said simply. "Don't say it." And he leaned in to kiss her on the cheek. She hugged him in return. Then she smiled and nodded as she turned and walked away, leaving him standing there with his basket and a big grin on his face.

Chapter 21

Anna found the Temple of Vesta where she had last left it. Incense continued to burn on its altar, just as it did the first day she had arrived. She lifted the hem of her tunic and ascended the steps to the portico that graced its façade. And weaving her way through the immense columns that stood guarding its entrance proudly, she walked inside and found the gilded mirror where she had last seen it, hanging on a far wall in the back corner of a chamber.

Ah, she thought, exhaling a deep breath, it was indeed a beautiful mirror. So exquisite and mysterious. She stood there for a little while, just staring at it. Strange how it seemed to stare right back at her. So many secrets lie within its depths, she thought. Then slowly she stepped up to the mirror and lifted her hand, placing it on the glass. She closed her eyes and waited, holding her breath unconsciously as she did so. Then peeking at the mirror once again, she saw its reflection change. There was the room in her grandmother's house from where Anna had first arrived. It was draped with white sheets over the walls and furniture in order to keep away the dust. And placing her hand on the gilded mirror once again, the glass gave way and disappeared. Then lifting the hem of her tunic, she stepped through its frame and into the room that lay within.

Anna turned back around to face her reflection after stepping through the mirror. Gone were the long tunic and the sandals that she had been wearing. Her favorite blue jeans, sneakers and navy sweatshirt now took their place. Her hair was also pulled back into a loose ponytail off her face. Anna just stood there for a little while, sagging a bit as she exhaled. She needed a moment to collect herself before leaving the room. Her grandmother would be home soon, and she would know. Baba would know that Anna had visited the gilded mirror once again, just by looking at Anna's face. She would know. Anna thought about this now, wondering what Baba knew about the mirror's history. She had never said very much about it, other than that it had traveled far and long. She was certainly right about that, Anna thought as she smiled to herself.

Anna picked up the long sheet that had covered the mirror before she had dropped it on the floor to step through its frame. She hung it carefully back over its surface, letting it drape over the glass. Then she remembered something. And pulling back one of the sleeves of her sweatshirt, she smiled in relief. There, on her wrist, hung the delicate silver bracelet that Cassius had given her. She closed her eyes for a moment, already missing her friend. It was poignant. Then she left the room, turning off the light and closing the door behind her.

The clock on the wall showed the exact time it had been when she had first entered the room. That seemed like so long ago. Strange how no time passed here, in the present. It was nice, actually. Very nice. How could she travel back in time otherwise? She couldn't, she realized. This mirror–this whole experience–was an amazing gift.

Anna walked back down the wide curving staircase in Baba's house. She wanted to try and read a little before her grandmother returned home. She got her bag that she had left on the table by the entrance. Then she went and sat down on a couch to read. But the words did not register. Nothing did. Her mind kept traveling back to Pompeii. She kept thinking about Cassius and all that had occurred to them there. What would have happened to Cassius and his father if she had not bumped into him that first day in the marketplace? Would they too have perished in the eruption as so many others had? And what of Claudius's renowned talents for painting beautiful frescoes? Would those artistic gifts have been lost and forgotten beneath the rubble?

Both Cassius and Claudius might very well have died, their lives like two flames cruelly snuffed out by fate; their bodies trapped in a moment of agony, and buried under the volcano's debris. But that did *not* happen, Anna kept reminding herself. No. They had escaped. She closed her eyes now, wondering about the life Cassius had made for himself after she had left him standing there under an arch of the colonnaded gallery, and if he had indeed followed in his father's footsteps as he had planned. It had been so hard to say goodbye to him. It's always hard to say goodbye. *Then don't say it,* he had told her, with his beautiful grin. "Alright Cass," she whispered aloud to the empty space around her. "I won't say it. I won't ever say it." And she smiled.

Epilogue

The eruption of Mount Vesuvius in AD 79 was a catastrophe of unprecedented proportions that literally rocked the ancient world. As it was the first time that the great volcano had erupted in about 700 years, none of the people living in the region of Campania by the modern day Bay of Naples in Italy had ever even heard of a volcano. They were, however, used to much seismic activity that occurred there. It was a rich and fertile land, lush with vines, orchards, and a variety of other thriving plant life that was largely due to the fruitfulness of the soil produced by the volcano itself.

Pompeii was a thriving resort town whose many inhabitants included wealthy Romans from the aristocracy and upper classes, merchants, and a service class comprised of slaves and paid servants. The earthquake of AD 63 had affected much damage to its public buildings, temples, water systems and houses, and evidence of extensive repairs could be seen from its excavations. But the people did not think much of the tremors that shook their town. Many indeed brushed them off with a wave of their hand. Little did they know that those tremors were related to the volcano that sat in their midst.

When Mount Vesuvius first erupted, people stared in wonder at the strange cloud that rose from its crater into the sky, totally oblivious to the danger. Although many people did escape during the early stage of the eruption, thousands did not. Winds carried the fallout south of Vesuvius, directly over Pompeii. It destroyed several other towns in the region as well including Herculaneum, Oplontis, Stabiae, and large sections of the beaches in the Bay of Naples, and the beautiful countryside to the east.

The eruption was preceded by several days of tremors until the great mountain finally blew its top, thrusting millions of tons of ash, pumice and lava many miles into the sky, where it spread out like an umbrella and blocked the sun for about two days. Ash and pumice rained down on the people. Then pyroclastic avalanches thundered down the side of Vesuvius like roaring waves of searing gases and rock at frightening speeds, which sealed the fates of those that might have survived the eruption's early stage. Volcanic activity continued for several days at least, smothering the town and all evidence of life. Titus Flavius Vespasianus, who was the emperor at the time of the eruption, provided generous relief assistance to the people who had fled with their lives, and subsequently settled in other provinces.

Mount Vesuvius erupted several more times over the course of the centuries after the terrible calamity of AD 79. And over time, the town of Pompeii was forgotten, buried under a charred and blackened desert that inadvertently preserved the Roman town for posterity. Before it was accidentally discovered by a farmer who was digging a well in the early eighteenth century, it was thought of simply as a legend, much like the lost city of Atlantis. Since then, excavations have uncovered one of history's most famous disasters, and are an especially invaluable insight into life in a Roman town in the first century AD.

But more than the town itself—with its impressive buildings and temples, colonnaded galleries, aqueducts and advanced plumbing systems, theaters, amphitheater, shops and taverns, fountains and shrines, sumptuous gardens, and stunning mosaics and frescoes—are its people. Especially those people who have been immortalized in their final moments of life, buried by the ash and fallout, and revealed to us through the famous plaster casts that have captured their imprints in such excruciating detail. These revelations are at once fascinating and heart-breaking. They are a poignant reminder of the terrible suffering that befell them, and the fragility of life everywhere. And this, above all, is perhaps what makes Pompeii live on with such resounding significance in the depths of our imaginations and within our hearts.

Printed in Great Britain
by Amazon.co.uk, Ltd.,
Marston Gate.